THE ENIGMA

BY AARON PERSAUD
ILLUSTRATION BY CONSTAN-LEROIS

THE SHADOW

"C'mon, Mekhi, what's stopping you?" Patrice spoke to me over the phone. "We need a good designer, and they sure as hell aren't gonna bump me down from storyboarding anytime soon."

"I know I *can* do it," I replied, fiddling with my keys to try and open my apartment door. "Just give me some time to think about it at least, is that okay?"

I finally got the key in the lock and let myself in.

"Of course," Patrice said. "I'll let you sleep on it and I'll wait for you to tell me tomorrow that you're up to the challenge."

I chuckled at her confidence. "Mm-hmm," I responded. "Well thank you again, as always, and I'll see you tomorrow."

"See ya! Night, night."

"Good night."

I hung up the phone, threw my shit onto the bed, followed then by myself, and stared at the ceiling.

Did it finally pay off? All those years of interning, studying, drawing, and scribbling during class as a kid and not even paying attention? Guess so.

Patrice was the leading storyboard artist on a new cartoon production for a prominent kids' network. Even I didn't have all the details as to what the plot or premise of the show was, but I knew that there was a lot of money being poured into the project. Larry Turner was the leading producer for the series, and if his resume said anything, the show was to be a hit based on reputation alone – quality aside.

In truth, I was being a little overly humble and modest to Patrice. Of course I could do it. I knew that without a doubt, and so did she. Her and I have known each other for a couple of years now. Between having my work commissioned and doing freelancing, Patrice was occupied with actual work in the industry shortly after graduating art school. She wasted no time, always quick to get ahead of the game while also keeping to herself. She even got me my first internship where I learned the ropes of working behind-the-scenes. Now, she was asking if I could serve as the lead character designer for the show. If it meant getting to work alongside her, I was all for it.

But I also didn't favor making such fast decisions. I wasn't going to be able to sleep easily the whole night. My mind would be racing. It was my first real gig after all. I stepped into my art studio, surrounded by the countless colorful designs plastered on the walls. They were creations over the years from when I was young, some recent, some I'd made on road trips when I was bored, some during study hall in school, and many more I don't remember exactly when they were made.

Sitting on my drawing board was an unfinished project I had started last night, but didn't get around to completing and probably won't anytime soon. It only possessed a head and shoulders, not even hair or eyes. I don't really know what it was supposed to be. A character, an object, an animal. Who knows? That's how my imagination worked. I just sort of drew whatever came to mind and went with it.

One of the pieces hung on my wall was my first drawing. Well, first *complete* drawing, I should mention. At least, that's what my mother said it was. And looking back on it, she always knew I would have a natural talent for art. I was four, I believe, and she said it was the best drawing she'd seen from any four-year-old. Any mother would think that of their child, I'm sure, but my friends and other relatives said the same.

It was a drawing of what I could only describe as perhaps a hybrid between a cute little bunny and a tiger cub. It had the features of a bunny, but the fur pattern of orange and black stripes. I like to think that was due to me watching Winnie the Pooh around that time, and having a special liking to Tigger. It was the only explanation I could think of. But as I was viewing it, for the first time, I spotted a rather minuscule but distractingly odd detail.

Near the bottom right corner of the paper was a small black speck. Why was that odd? On a piece of paper over 20 years old in which wear and tear were bound to occur? Well, I bet anyone would be amazed at how well-kept this drawing was after such time had passed. The paper was never that dirty or dusty, yet for some reason, I was just now noticing this one little detail left behind. A little spot…

It was too perfect, too intentional. Oh sure, I just put it there myself when I first drew it as a child. That was the probable explanation. Kids do weird things like that sometimes. Maybe I just felt the need to put a little mark with my pencil or pen and left it there where no one but myself would notice. Then again, nothing else on the paper reflected black whatsoever, and it was entirely in crayon. What might've caused that? Was it believable that I had a random pencil or pen just lying around at the time? It's plausible. But why would I have done that? I kept trying to contemplate in my head what my four-year-old self might've been thinking, to the point of overthinking myself, but how the hell would I know? I was a pretty weird kid and it was such a distant memory.

Maybe that was my way of signing my art when I was that age, you know? Signed here, Mekhi Phillips, in a black dot. That's how you knew it was me-

What the hell was I doing? I had sleep to catch up on.

Patrice had convinced me, and by the next two days, I was sketching new ideas for the show and working closely with her. I was coming up with character designs while she and a few others constructed building layouts, suggesting what sort of colors and contrasts to use that might better capture the essence and tone of the series (a mainly action/adventure genre with some lighthearted comedy trickled throughout, as I'd come to learn). I felt at times that I was overstepping my bounds, but Patrice would let me know. I soon learned that it was a more collaborative effort in creating an animated series than most would have you think. More ideas were better than little in the art director's eyes. At least, that's what Patrice would have led me to think.

I finished the first draft for the lead character of the show, a minimalistic cartoon style reminiscent of Bruce Timm's illustrations. I cleared it with Patrice for her approval, and to my pleasure, she loved it. She said she'd pitch it up to the art director, Brad, as well, and then onto the higher-ups (producers) for final review to make sure that they, too, were pleased. Everything had to please them, at the end of the day. Not most audiences understood that about the business. You might make great art, but it means nada if the men at the top don't see a profit out of it.

I was just wrapping up for the day and was getting ready to leave the studio when Brad himself came by to talk to me, Patrice at his side. Reading her expression, she looked neither happy nor upset, but somewhere in the grey area.

"Hey, 'Ki," Brad called to me. That was my nickname, 'Ki.

"Hey," I said back.

"So, bad news, and some good news."

"Oh…"

"Want me to give you the good news first?"

"Mmm, I prefer bad news first."

I gave Patrice a brief glance, to which she returned a subtle microexpression, signaling to me that the news would be much less than favorable.

"Cool," Brad continued. "Well, the bad news is that Larry thinks we should change the design to more… eh, how do I put it… *minimal*?"

I arched my brow. Technically, Larry had the final say over all creative decisions, including Brad or myself.

"It already is minimalist," I politely argued. "That's the form, anyways."

"I know, and trust me, man, it looks great," Brad insisted. "If it were up to me, I'd definitely keep it, but unfortunately, the guys up the chain aren't one hundred percent satisfied. Say, more like 85 percent."

They could draw it themselves then, I wanted to say. But instead said, "Alright, I'll, uh, start thinking of some new drafts and I'll show you them in the morning."

"Nah, don't lose any sleep over it. We'll work on it throughout the week and next week. Sound good?" I nodded. He then nudged Patrice. "I know this one here'll keep you on your toes, yeah?"

Patrice forced a small laugh to help ease the tension that was apparent.

"Good. Hey, man, sorry again to be the bearer of bad news. It's nothing personal, it's not an attack on you as an artist, it's just they want something just a little more to par with what *their* vision for the show is."

I gave the fakest reply probably in my entire life. "I completely understand," I said with a smile. "It's nothing. And oh yeah, what was the good news?"

Brad looked thrown off for a bit but then regained his thought. "Oh, the good news?" he said. "Well, you get another shot."

He gave a cheeky sort of smile that for the first time since meeting him, I had a tempting urge, similar to a bad itch, that I could knock those perfect white teeth out of his face.

14

...

That night I got home and did the opposite of what Brad said, and stayed up working on different sketches and ideas for new designs for the character. What was wrong with mine? I thought it was a timeless animation design and easy on the eyes. Not only that, but from a creative perspective, it worked for the show. I knew exactly what they wanted, too. Some boggled-down simplistic carbon copy design that'd been done many times before. The storyboard art was better than that. Patrice was better than that. I figured it was time to try something unique and fresh once again, while simultaneously being a callback to the old animation myself and other generations before me grew up on. Appreciation for effort seems to be dead these days.

It was an hour past midnight now, and I didn't leave my drawing board for hours. I didn't get up to use the bathroom, get a glass of water, or anything. But whilst drowning myself in my work, I did peek over again at my first drawing posted on the wall to my left, and I noticed something that made me squint to make sure my eyes weren't deceiving me.

I got up to go over and check for a closer look, and my eyes saw just fine. The dot I'd seen in the bottom right corner of the paper was in a different position this time. It'd moved upwards and more towards the left side of the page. Again, I was tired, this time from my own will, but I couldn't have been that exhausted to see that I was completely right.

And another thing I observed, but perhaps was also tripping over due to my lack of sleep. The spot was slightly bigger this time, and more akin to a filled circle. First, it was as if someone planted a single dab with their pen, whereas here it was more of a jot and two little rotations with the ball.

The next afternoon during lunch, I showed Brad what I'd come up with for the new character designs. I showed him four different alternatives for what we might use. I watched his face change from wide-eyed, amused, confused, and bemused in one sitting.

"I think this one will do," he said, pointing to the first one.

It was the most simplistic of the drawings, and in my opinion, my most uninspired piece. Of course, he'd pick that one.

"What about this one?" I pointed out another. "This one has more emphasis on his facial expression and gives him a bit more emotion, you know?"

"Yeah, but we can't have the characters stand too far out from each other," Brad said. "The differences in colors will be what distinguishes them, in this case."

But character designs were so much more than just color. Expressions of the face told a thousand words about who the person or thing was that you were drawing. Nevertheless, I agreed with him, though, not in my best interest.

Gazing later that night at the other drafts I'd whipped up sitting on my drawing board in my room, I sighed with pity at the wasted time and threw them in the trash can. Whilst doing so, I glanced over at my old drawing again to see where the mystery dot might've ended up this time. I'd almost forgot about it earlier in the day, possibly due to how ridiculous of an assumption it was to assume a dot could magically change places across a piece of paper.

I discovered that it was in the same position I last found it, however, something was unusual yet again. Getting a closer look, I found that it seemed not only bigger, but I could almost swear it was beginning to appear more than just a measly spot and an entirely different shape instead. But it was too small to see with my naked eye.

I took a magnifying glass from my desk and placed it a good distance between my eye and the paper. I squinted with my right to get a good look at what I was seeing. It didn't make sense. It *was* a shape. A shape of some sort of figure. A person, I could've sworn. It was a black silhouette of a humanoid shape, and it looked to be in amazing detail for it to be so shrimpy. I just knew that if I could somehow put a microscope over it, I could get a completely detailed and intricate picture.

It was so strange. It hadn't been a dot after all. It was a vivid picture. But how? I couldn't have drawn that as a kid. Not at that age. Even for an adult or any skilled artist, it was practically impossible. It was unimaginably impressive to draw something of that detail in that size.

I tried to see what sort of expression or stance the figure was doing, though, with close inspection, it didn't seem to be doing much at all. It sort of just stood there, and it was just a shadow where I couldn't see any sort of emotion on its face whatsoever. However, the more I stared at it, the more I noticed it began to unsettle me. It was so out there, so far-fetched for it to even exist right there on the paper. And the question still bugged me, how did it even get there in the first place?

•••

The next day I was off, and I decided to call my mom. I knew she'd probably have a picture of it somewhere in her photo albums.

"How's the new job going?" she asked me over the phone, excitedly.

"It's goin'," I told her. "How's the blood pressure?"

"Oh, I'm keeping it at a good level right now. Doctor says to eat less red meat, so I've been working on that."

"You must be struggling."

"Eh, it's not as bad as I thought it'd be. There's days I'll still want a burger here and there, but there's plenty of other good things to cook that don't have all that junk in it."

"Yeah, but then there's using too much butter and seasoning, knowing you."

"Exactly."

I then changed the subject. "Hey, do you remember my first drawing?" I shot the question.

"Uh, well, I remember a lot of your drawings," she replied. "Your first drawing?"

"Yeah, the one I took with me? It used to be on the fridge all the time."

"Oh, yeah, the crayon-colored one?"

"Mm-hmm."

"Yeah, I remember that one. What about it?"

"I know this is random, but I was wondering if you had a picture of it anywhere in one of the photo albums or somewhere. There's a small little detail drawn on the picture that I swore wasn't there the first time I drew it. I just wanna be sure, out of curiosity, you know?"

"Hmm, I may have it somewhere. Hold on…"

She and I talked a bit more while she looked around through the photo books for the old drawing. She knew she'd taken a picture of it somewhere. That's what she told herself. She usually did with these kinds of things just in case they ever got lost. My mother was also from the generation where photos weren't exactly scarce but also held with more value which captured special memories and moments to last a lifetime, compared to nowadays where it's easier than ever to take a photo, giving less need and maybe want for a photo album. It was a good trip down memory lane for her, as she would make warm-hearted comments and exclamations of joy as she spoke of all the old photos she'd turn the page over and find, whether they were baby pictures of me and my siblings or old family vacation trips.

Eventually, she struck gold. "Well whaddya know," she said. "I found it."

"Wow," I replied. "I'm actually surprised it was that easy."

"That's why I keep telling you to start getting a photo album so you can have these memories kept forever. And you can keep one for all your drawings, too."

"I do have one for all my drawings."

"I'm not just talking about a portfolio, but like an actual photo book, so you can show your kids and my grandkids one day."

"If I have kids."

"Ha-ha, gimme some hope, won't you? I'll send you the picture."

"Thanks, Ma."

"You're welcome, baby. Love you."

"Love you, too."

When she did send it, I paid close attention to the detail in the photo she'd sent compared to the one on the wall. Everything was practically the same, except for one thing. The silhouette wasn't drawn on the photo my mom sent. It was only on the actual copy. So I was right, I didn't actually draw that. I knew I couldn't have. Then who?

I decided to set up a camera one night to check and make sure no one was breaking in. It was a cheap studio apartment and I didn't have the money and consent with my landlord just yet to install ADT or some alternative. Crazy enough, the thought of someone breaking into my apartment just to add an elaborate illustration was hilarious by itself, but still no less creepy. What would be the reason? Just a harmless prank from one of the guys at the studio? Patrice had no way of getting into my place, even though she's been over many times. I couldn't think of who, and I couldn't imagine going through the trouble of trying to pull something like that off, let alone risking a criminal offense for trespassing. Even still, the impossible and precise detail of the figure didn't seem realistic from a measly creep in the night.

That next day I looked at the drawing to find that the silhouette appeared slightly bigger than last time. Now it was starting to get quite unsettling. I had to review the footage. But what I saw led me nowhere. No one broke in. Nothing was different from the paper on camera. Everything remained unchanged. For whatever reason, what was seen through the lens didn't reflect what I was seeing in reality.

•••

A couple months had passed and by the end of the pre-production, I had finalized most of the character sketches, and by then, the characters were, for the most part, set on their final designs. Or rather, as final as *final* can get. The voice actors would need to record their lines, then the animators would come in to orchestrate the movements to match the speech patterns along with character expressions, and the eventual pilot would still need to be screened of course for review so we could get a consensus on what does and doesn't work with the show. But for now, all else was nearly wrapped up. I hadn't noticed a change in the silhouette since that night I checked the footage. I just accepted that it would be a permanent mark on my first drawing ever. While it bothered me a little, at least my mother had the original copy saved in our family photos.

I'd gotten home again and walked into my studio room and nearly jumped at the sight on the wall. The silhouette was no longer miniature but now grown in size, taking up nearly a quarter of the page. The texture of the grain or ink drawn into the page bore a stark presence, almost as though it were burned into the paper. It contrasted with the bright vibrant crayon colors aside from it in a morbid fashion with a nightly black hue.

I stepped over to the paper nervously, afraid of some unknown threatening aura that could now be felt within the room. Getting a closer look, the silhouette was filled with the most absolute darkest of shades I'd ever seen, like staring into a black hole, but one other striking detail was now apparent that gave me chills. I could discern that the figure held an actual expression on its face this time. A calm sinister smirk.

I grabbed the paper off the wall and put it away in one of the bottom drawers in the studio room. The last thing I wanted to do was to see that thing every day I walked past it.

That night I slept well up until about 2 or 3 AM when suddenly I thought I heard a noise from within the studio room. It sounded like tapping or light banging against the walls or drawers. I got up from my room and crept into the kitchen first to grab a knife, then sneaked over to the room. The door was already open. I'd have to flip the switch to see who was inside if anyone. Fuck, I hoped there wasn't anyone.

I cautiously turned on the light to the room, the illumination straining my eyes, and then quickly scanned the area. Nobody. A sigh of relief came over me, and then I suddenly felt silly for getting worked up over nothing. I then looked down at the drawer that I discarded the drawing in, glaring at it for a moment. Why not, I thought.

I put the knife down on the dresser and kneeled to open the drawer, grabbing the handle. The sight of it from last time was so eerie, yet alluring. But I had already considered throwing it away ever since it became a noticeable presence, so I figured I might as well do just that since it was giving me all this trouble.

My hand pulled on the dresser handle, and it opened to reveal that malicious smirk now covering the entire page, the size of an actual head, staring directly into my soul. I jumped back onto the floor and froze for a bit. The eyes, and the face… and my old drawing. It was gone. I couldn't even see it anymore. It had been replaced with whatever this thing was.

After getting myself together, I immediately burned it with the grill outside on my balcony. Burned it to bits and discarded them over into the grass. I watched it disappear into the night, still shaking from that god awful sight. I might as well have killed an old friend, a piece of my memories.

I thought to myself, at least I had the original, though, if not the physical copy. But when I looked back at the message my mom had sent me of the picture, it was gone. It appeared as though the file had been corrupted or something and I was unable to view it. I had saved it in my gallery on my phone as well right after she sent it, but still, it was nowhere in sight. Like it never existed.

I tried asking my mom the next day if she could try sending it again, but to her and my surprise, the photo was ruined. Somehow, the image was blurred and awfully distorted to where it was unintelligible. She didn't spill anything on it and nothing could've possibly tainted the photo from where she placed the album, she told me, as none of the other pictures were at all affected. There was really no way to explain it, it… just sort of died. That was the only copy she had. The last living proof of it even existing.

•••

Later that day, I hung out and had a couple of drinks with Patrice and some friends of ours and pretty much went through a mild five stages of grief within one evening. I felt like a piece of me was now gone from losing the picture, but I knew that there were countless more creations to be made and hundreds that I *did* create. That was the beauty of art, I told myself in a drunken slurred speech to my buddies, that art perseveres and is forever in all aspects. Or some sentimental shit like that, I don't really remember, I was plastered.

Patrice took me home that night and made sure I got inside my place safely. Still inebriated, I stumbled into my room to undress, but first, decided to make a trip to the studio room. I turned on the light and looked around at the various other projects I'd made over the years, soaking in my vanity, glory, and pride.

"How 'bout that, huh?" I said aloud to no one. "Huh? How's that? And there's more where that came from."

It was my big 'F You' to the silhouette and to the loss of my first accomplishment. I didn't know who I was trying to prove myself to or what, but that didn't matter. I was so out of it and couldn't even see the hangover that was about to hit me in the morning anyway.

As I was turning to leave the room, I took a glimpse of one of the other drawings that put me in first place for an art contest back in fourth grade. It was a spin on Salvador Dali's *Persistence of Memory*, you know, the one with the melting clocks? It was my favorite painting, and I decided to do one of my own, but with a warped depiction of my bedroom at the time. In it, my bed was melting into the floor, the trophies and toys on my dresser liquifying bit by bit, the windowpane seemed to turn flimsy, some of the walls were even oozing. I even drew it to where you could see a bit of my bathroom door open and some of the inside, like the mirror, sink, toilet, shower. Some of those objects were also starting to melt. And inside of the bathroom, you could even see the shape of someone hiding… a shadow.

I sobered up real quick again. I know I didn't draw that. I know for a goddamn fact that I didn't draw that there. With the help of my magnifying glass again, I aimed over the bathroom door cracked open in the drawing. I watched the silhouette stare directly back at me through the mirror, with that same expression. That devilish smirk.

•••

About a year passed, and as we were wrapping up production on the cartoon, I was offered a position as a character designer for another upcoming animated series. My work had impressed the many higher-ups and Patrice had put in a good word for me. It seemed like a dream come true, in otherwise more favorable circumstances. However, I wasn't drawing like I used to. I sketched here and there, but I didn't have time anymore. I'd also assisted in managing and overseeing other artists' work, micromanaging and dictating what passes as art or not. Taking note of that passion, that fire in their young, hungry eyes… it was like ripping a plant from its roots.

By the end, there had been only one picture left in my studio that wasn't tainted by the shadow. A self-portrait of me in an animated style. I stared at it with a cold, desolate visage. I didn't even recognize it anymore. I remember a time where I might've been proud of making something this grand, but now I don't know what to feel. It didn't mean anything to me anymore. And in the far distance of the background on the canvas, there I could glimpse the bastard waiting. With the magnifying glass zoomed in on it, it stood there, with its arms crossed, head tilted down with that dubious grin, staring at me. It knew. It knew good and well what it was. A malevolent force with intentions unbeknownst to me.

It was no use in waiting for the shadow to take its full form and completely devour the drawing with no remorse, as it did with the others. They'd all been lost, with no way of ever recovering them. No recollections of pictures, files, videos, nothing. All disappeared from the face of the universe. And with that, I decided to do the honor myself, and burn the last one standing.

I went back to my studio room, staring at the empty walls around me. They'd once been plastered with creations of grandeur, zest, creativity, and most importantly, individuality. I was 28-years-old and didn't even recognize who I was anymore.

I could no longer perceive it with my own eyes, but I just felt its presence. I knew somewhere, looming over me from a dimension invisible to myself, that it was still watching me, glaring at me with that same mischievous, hungry smirk.

ABYSMAL

"No peeking still," my husband nagged, his hands still over my eyes as he guided me.

"How can I peek with your hands literally over my face," I remarked. He chuckled.

After what felt like forever with him making sure I didn't bump into anything up to the mystery destination, my husband Jackson assured me that we were finally there. Thank God...

"Alright, open up!" he said as he unveiled his hands from my face.

Now that we were here, I felt the rush of excitement again, and a shy yet exuberant grin grew over my face as I slowly opened my eyes. Once they opened, however, they widened tenfold at the sight before me.

"Whoa," I exclaimed.

Jackson chuckled. "Soooo, did I pick out a good birthday gift or what?" he teased.

It was truly a sight to behold. An underwater luxury hotel suite, with all the delicacies and comfort a guest could dream of, encased entirely in an underwater tank with a view to die for at nearly every angle. Undoubtedly, it was a great birthday gift.

"Baby, this is amazing," I spoke. I turned to look at him. "I-I was just kinda joking when I said bring me the ocean if you could, you know?"

He and the usher who led us to the room with our luggage exchanged laughs.

"You should know by now I take almost everything you say literally," Jackson said as he stepped my way, towering over me by merely two inches.

"Mmm-hmm," I uttered through my smile, and we both leaned in for a kiss.

The usher rolled our luggage over to the king-sized bed (really, it looked even bigger than king-sized) and neatly set them to the side.

"Happy birthday," Jackson said.

"Thanks, Babe," I replied, as we both went in for another kiss. Poor usher, I thought. I know it must've been awkward for him right about now.

"Um, sorry to intrude," the gentleman noted, "But if you two would like, the kitchen staff has prepared a lovely four-course lunch, which should be about ready in the next 30 to 40 minutes?"

"Oh," I uttered.

"Nice," Jackson followed. "What do you think?" he asked me. "I'm famished."

I gave him a crazy look. "Shit yeah," I replied under my breath, but quite loudly. I noticed the usher, "Oops, I mean-", clearing my throat, "Yes, my husband and I would love to attend," changing my whole demeanor.

Him and I both chuckled like idiot children. That's simply how we were together. Like children. Though, when it was time to be adults, I was usually the parent in the relationship. He was a messy eater, I used proper dining etiquette. He needed a haircut, I did it for him. He got bruised up or injured doing God-knows-what, I fixed him up. He wants to travel to a random city over the weekend, I do all the planning (except this time, to my surprise).

Jackson was smart - very smart... but dumb at the same time. He was like a golden retriever. Had lots of energy and charisma, always the center of everyone else's attention, yet, he couldn't hold his own to save his life. Extremely all over the place. In a way, however, that's what I find attractive about him. His zest for life and a childlike curiosity outlasting his years. I liked to have my fun as well, don't get me wrong. But I was more Virgo-like in my ways, even though I'm a Pisces myself.

...

Lunch was held in the hotel's center aquarium, giving us a full view of the ocean around us. Glass surrounded us with a bright blue luminescence as the sun reflected light through the large sea.

We were presented with a lovely four-course meal of seafood selections. Both of us got the seafood chowder as a starter. I got spicy Caribbean shrimp and he got oysters for appetizers. For the entrees, I got a nice big baked salmon, and Jackson got a huge lobster tail with a side of melted butter and mashed potatoes. It was all delicious, needless to say, and to top it all off, we had carb-packed tall slices of strawberry cheesecake. I could barely get up from the table after we were done.

After congratulating the head chef for such a fine meal, Jackson shot the question.

"Where are all the fish?" he asked.

It was one of those things I didn't even think to ask, yet it was so obvious. Where were the fish? I didn't know we were coming here until just a while ago. Had I not seen any pictures from the brochures in our room, I'd think this place didn't have any fish at all. It was a good question.

"Ah, the fish," the chef said. "They're usually out most of the day and usually at night, they'll obviously be harder to see and go elsewhere. But today must be one of those days where they'll just sorta hide."

"Hide?" I remarked.

"Yes," the chef said. "Mostly from predators, if they're around. But that's strange, there usually aren't any around. There's the sharks, but even still, nothing that's a serious threat to make the others leave."

"There's sharks here?" Jackson asked in a tone that I couldn't tell was either amazed or afraid.

"Oh yes, a couple of them will show up from time to time. No great whites, or hammerheads, or anything crazy of the sort, but yes, there are a few."

"Hmm," Jackson uttered.

"Well, hopefully they turn up soon," I added. "We gotta get some pictures, right Babe?"

I nudged Jackson at his side, to which he didn't noticeably return much of a reaction.

"Mm-hmm," he noised passively.

Maybe he was starting to get a food coma, too, and needed to lay down. I know I did. We'd gotten back to the room and did exactly that.

•••

After a pleasant nap, I woke up to the magical view of the suite being illuminated with hidden LED lights outlining the bed, walls, and other pieces of large furniture. The room held a bright gold luminescence along with the now dark blue to almost pitch black abyss of the ocean. I wonder if that was something that could be turned off or it just stayed like that. Either way, I wasn't complaining one bit.

Jackson woke up not too long after, and I barely saw him shuffle over to the bathroom in a hurry, as I was on my phone with my back turned. Was he sick?

"You all right, Babe?" I called to him.

"Yeah," Jackson replied. "Had to piss."

Oh, well that made sense. With that, I turned on camera mode for my phone, and began snapping random pictures, and was getting ready to do a panorama view. I had the lens set at one side of the room, starting at the edge of the first wide window, then began to drag across the room. I made it past the first window, then past the walls and door to the bathroom occupied by Jackson, then to the other side window, and was about to come around to the end of the last huge display behind me, until I noticed something through the lens.

I lowered my phone to get a look with my own eyes and saw that there was an enormous shadow of space outside the glass. It could've been the lack of sunlight reflecting down on that particular spot, but then I thought, was it really that dark already? It was only a half 'til six, so it made sense for the water to be dark, but not *that* dark. The thing was, it stood out from the rest of the area like a sore thumb. You could still tell apart the ocean floor from other sections of the room, as well as the tiny rocks at the bottom. But over in this particular spot, it was near-total blackness. An abnormally large disquieting contrast in the area around it. Maybe it was just a large rock structure. Like a fjord, maybe? No, those are like mountains or something, I think.

Then I heard the toilet flush. I waited for Jackson to come back out, but a couple of moments kept passing longer than expected. I was getting suspicious again.

"You sure you're okay?" I called again.

"Yeah," he answered.

It would make sense if he got sick from the food, perhaps. It was seafood, after all, and that among other recipes could have a tendency to make anyone's stomach queasy if not properly prepared. But *I* didn't have any issues so far. We ate nearly the same thing, as we picked from each other's plates all the time.

I went ahead and gave him another minute, but as more time kept passing and I didn't hear from him, I decided that was it.

"Hey, I gotta piss, too," I announced, as I got up and started approaching the door.

No response. Then, a few seconds later, "Okay," I heard him respond. Weird, I thought.

I slowly turned the knob and opened the door slowly, as not to budge right in. To my confusion, he wasn't in the bathroom anymore at all. Huh?

"Jackson?" I called for him.

I looked across and saw that there was another door leading to a different room, or closet maybe? It was cracked open.

I went over and swung open the door to find a nice tidy compartmentalized space, the only room that wasn't encased in glass, with Jackson loafing around. It had a nice window seat cushion that extended along the side of the walls of the entire room, and a circular window that simply showed the outside view of the ocean, which was also nearly pitch black as the shadow that cast over near the bedside window I'd a moment ago. Perhaps I was right. It was just large boulders or rocky structures blocking the light on those specific sides of the glass.

"You know this wouldn't be a bad room to crash in," he said, as he kept aimlessly searching around for something.

"I guess not?" I awkwardly replied.

"Could be a good place to do… other things, too, yeah?"

"It's kind of a tight space, don't you think?"

"We've managed with worse."

"You know, there is a whole bed back there," I said, pointing my finger to the door.

"Yeah…" Then his mind trailed off elsewhere before he looked at me again. "I'm done in the bathroom. You said you needed to go, right?"

I gave him a certain look. "I lied," I answered. "You okay?"

"Why wouldn't I be?" he responded, but I knew when he was playing clueless.

"You've been acting kinda strange since lunch."

"Oh?"

"I mean, we both know you're strange as it is, but… earlier you seemed sort of all right, but now since the sun is starting to come down, I don't even know."

"True," he said, still not actually paying attention as he was still searching around the room.

I was getting a little fed up. "What are you looking for?" I asked.

"Something to cover this window with," he said. "Can we get seasick from this? You know, with us being underwater and everything?"

"… Maybe?"

"There's nothing but towels and a bunch of useless crap in here - are there any like really big pillows out there in the bedroom?"

My gosh, he was acting strange. The obvious question came next.

"Why do you need to cover the window?" I asked.

"Because… I don't want anyone spying on us," he answered.

"Really?"

"Yeah."

"We're underwater."

"I noticed."

"Who's gonna spy on us? The fish? There aren't any."

"You don't know, there might be people with submarines or something down here trying to capture a couple of lovebird guests having a good ole time down here to sell on the internet or who-knows-what."

"Okay, one, I'm not screwing you in this room, and two, what is going on with you? You're just acting so weird. What's wrong?"

He looked around nervously, biting his lip like a child keeping a dirty little secret. Then, he finally fessed up.

"I have… thalassophobia," he guiltily admitted.

"What?"

"Thalassophobia."

"What's that?"

"Fear of the ocean. Like deep water, all the shit that lurks in it, you know? Being stranded at sea, even. I've always been afraid of the water, babe. I tried to work on it, believe me, but nah. It's just always been that one thing I can't get over."

I was dumbfounded. "Wh-" I started, trying to find where to even begin. "You have a fear of the ocean and you booked us an underwater hotel with literally a 360 view of open water?"

His face was red. "Yeah," he muttered.

"Why?" I asked.

"'Cause, it was for you. It wasn't about me. I wanted you to be happy, and I wanted to get you something nice for your birthday, something I knew you'd love."

It was one of the many sweetest things I'd ever heard him say that I almost forgot how dumb he initially sounded at this moment. I went over to him and gently cupped his face with both my hands, my back facing the window now and his facing the door.

"Okay," I started, "Baby, you didn't have to get me anything - though, I'm very grateful for all of this. And besides, I still don't want you to be uncomfortable even if I'm not. We're   you know, a marriage. A unity, or whatever. A team. I wouldn't do something for you if I didn't like it either."

Jackson arched a brow.

"Okay, that came out very wrong. Of course, I'd make sacrifices for you, too. But you get my point?"

Then I realized he wasn't reacting to what I said at all, and was looking across the room past me towards the glass.

"The rock is gone," he whispered.

"Hmm?" I uttered.

I turned to face where he was looking and saw what he meant. The black abyss of space beyond the glass was no longer there, and instead, we saw the faint

blue glistening of the evening once again. Strange…
it'd been black as night a moment ago, I thought.
But Jackson said the same thing I was thinking. He,
too, thought it was a rock.

I looked to him. "Tell you what, I'll order us some
drinks - you pick - and I'll bring them back and we
can just hang out here, okay?"

His face lit up with excitement again. "You don't
have to do that, Babe? Don't let me ruin your b-
day."

"To me, it's ruined if you're not happy."

•••

I'd gotten room service to order us a tray of
varied alcoholic beverages (only under his card,
Jackson insisted). Champagne, Moscato, Grey
Goose, and a few other cocktails, along with some
crackers and cheeses to go along. We were soon to
get wasted. We hung out together in the small
enclosed room with our backs facing the window
atop a fortress of pillows I pulled from the master
bedroom and threw into the other room. I even
fulfilled his request to cover the window with other
stacks of pillows and whatever else I could find so
he wouldn't have to look outside.

We cuddled in the pillow fort we'd made and watched a movie on his tablet. Any other person might view this as a complete downer to their vacation, but for me, I actually enjoyed every second of it. We never usually partook in high-end sort of living activities, even with me thoroughly planning and making sure we budget down to a T, so they usually ended up like this instead where we much preferred the comfort of doing things the unconventional way, such as sleeping in another room aside from the bed on a stack of pillows. Plus, it made Jackson feel better, and he was usually always braver than me. For once, I saw a true vulnerability in him.

"We've been to the pool and stuff together," I said.

"Mm-hmm," he replied. He drank way more than me. He'd answer anything at this point.

"You didn't seem scared then."

"The pool isn't scary, the ocean is. Remember though, I couldn't go past six feet?"

Then I thought about it. He was right. He never went too far to the deep end of any pools we got in, nor did he bother to step as much as a single toe into the ocean when we visited the beach.

"Huh," I expressed. "I never noticed 'til now."

We kept on watching the movie for a couple more seconds before I had the urge to ask more questions.

"What about it scares you the most?" I asked.

He shrugged. "I mean, a lot of things. Like the thought of how deep it is… you never know what could be down there - here. The feeling of being surrounded by a vast bunch of endlessness, and being so small…" He shivered with chills. "Yeesh. Fuck that."

"Yeah, when you put it that way, that does sound pretty scary."

"Nah, you love it. You and the ocean have a pact."

"What?" I smiled.

"Admit it, you would love to be a little mermaid just swimmin' along in the abyss, waving at seamen - haha, *seamen* - passing by on their little boats and just having a grand time-"

"Oh shut up!" I laughed.

"-Just floating around with your long red hair collecting seashells singing, 'Unda da sea!'-"

"Whatever!"

"-Unda da seaaaa!"

He was hysterical, and we were both having a good time. At least he was enjoying himself now, much thanks to the alcohol, of course.

I had to get up and use the bathroom, for real this time. After doing so, I decided to go get my phone that I'd left on the charger from the bed. But when I stepped into the room, it was nearly pitch black. I couldn't see a damn thing.

What happened to the LED lights? Did they automatically turn off by themselves? It'd be weird if they did, though, because it wasn't at our discretion to do it ourselves, and who's to say we still needed the light or not?

I decided to use the bathroom light by swinging the door wide open to let the rest seep into the room and illuminate. Now, I could discern where everything was, if only faintly.

I went over to the bedside and pulled my phone from the USB. 100-percent battery life. Nice. While I was over there, I also turned on the lamplight perched next to me, and saw that it emitted a bright enough radiance to fill the entire corner of the bedroom. Might as well leave it on.

Then a thought occurred to me to check on the vast space I'd spotted earlier through the window. It would be directly in front of me. So I lifted my head to take a look, and to my stupidity, of course, it was indistinguishable now at this time of night. Some hours had passed since I last saw it, making the entire perspective a dark blue tint.

Though I loved the ocean and all the creatures that inhabited it, after hearing Jackson's opposing view on the subject, in a weird sense, I was now starting to get what he meant. The vast darkness of the underwater. The endless abyss. I could imagine how terrifying it must be to swim in such a colossal space with no sense of direction, no other object in sight. No way out...

And what made it more frightening, I think, wasn't that the water was pitch black. No, it was the fact that it was nearly complete darkness, but not entirely. You could observe the murkiness of the depths shift from light blue to an uncanny shaded indigo. Were the shadows underneath simply an indication of how far the light could reach from above? Or, could it be that something waited - patiently - down below?

Geez, I could have quite the imagination when I got to thinking too much by myself. I was even getting scared at my own thoughts. But if anything, I could now sympathize with my husband's dread.

I turned to walk back to the bathroom door when another thought struck me, stopping me in my tracks. The rock Jackson and I noticed earlier, or at least what we thought was a rock... wasn't it black? Like, entirely black? Black as night? And we both thought we were seeing things, where the rock had suddenly moved and we couldn't identify it anymore through the window of the back room. It was hard to say if it was a bad memory or the alcohol, but I could swear...

I went over to the telephone next to the bed and decided to call room service again.

"Front desk, how can I help you?" the female clerk on the other line answered.

"Hi, yes, I was just calling because I noticed the lights in our room aren't working anymore. Not the main lights for the lamp and bathroom and stuff, but for the LED lights, you know?"

"Oh, I see. Yes, there's a switch on the wall right next to the thermostat where you can turn them on. It has a knob where you can adjust the brightness, and another one that lets you change the color to whichever one you'd like also."

I shifted my eyes over to where she was referring to and found exactly what she meant. I could've found that if I bothered to look first.

"Oh, I see it now," I laughed. "I guess I'll check and make sure it's on or off."

"Sure, no worries," the clerk sounded pleased. "But that's strange. They normally stay on unless of course, the guests decide to shut them off or when they automatically shut off at sunrise."

"Hmm… maybe there was just a short power outage?" I suggested, though, it was probably unrealistic.

"Could be," the clerk fancied. "But either way, hopefully you and your husband can enjoy the lovely moonlight from above as well."

I was confused. "Moonlight?" I said.

"Yes. From where your room should be, it's placed in the perfect spot for the moon to be seen from the top of the glass."

"Really?" I replied, very puzzled. I looked up to see if I could maybe notice it through the top. "I don't see any-"

At the sight I was now witnessing, I felt every bone, every muscle, every nerve in my body turn cold. There was something on top of the glass. Not just on top, but engulfing the entire tank. Above were faint details of what I could only imagine was its mouth. It was circular almost, with rows of what looked like razor-sharp teeth getting smaller at the center.

"Hello?" the clerk said on the other line.

I couldn't move. A sensation more than just fear overcame me. I was petrified. At this moment, I never felt so small.

Then, the creature began to shift its entire body away from the glass, sending a near-seismic rumble throughout the suite. I dropped the phone onto the floor, and I followed suit as I got down, raising my arms as an instinctual reaction to try and shield me from whatever was about to happen next - as *if* that would do anything. I was in the presence of something further up the food chain than myself. Further up than any other predator that I knew that walked or swam the face of the earth.

As it released its grip from off the glass, shapes of monstrous tentacles began to flail about, leaving behind a powerful swooshing noise through the water, along with a resonant sound that the only way I could describe it as is something that couldn't be replicated. Not on this planet. It was deafening, earth-shattering, like something from a different world.

MuuuUUUuuuuuh

MuUUUuuuUUUUUUUuuh

It was so alien-like. It seemed to be coming from the thing itself. So powerful, even more so than the call of a blue whale or the roar of an earthquake. It was truly one of the loudest sounds I'd ever heard.

Suddenly, pure blackness no longer surrounded the view, as shades of the natural lighting of the ocean floor began to form again, and instantaneously, a white glow emitted from the glass ceiling. There it was. The moon. It had been there the whole time... and so had this thing.

As the creature rose higher away from my perspective, I was starting to get an even better look at its size. I still couldn't even grasp its entire shape. It was huge. A behemoth of an unknown force lurking down here, waiting to be discovered.

I was amazed, astonished even, but not in a positive manner. The same sensation kept overtaking me as I began to curl up into a ball next to the bed. The sensation that I'd never felt so small...

I planned on staying there and hiding under the bed until it was gone. Then I'd be safe. But Jackson...

I got up and immediately ran towards the bathroom and over into the other room, shutting the door behind me. He was still lying against the pillows watching the movie on his phone, not noticing a thing about what lies beyond the glass. I couldn't have been the only one to hear it, I thought.

"Baby," I panicked.

He looked at me, concerned. "What's wrong?" he asked. I guess he didn't hear what I did after all.

But I couldn't tell him, I thought. I was already scared as it was, but telling him might be catastrophic, and he'd never want to leave this room.

"I-I…" I stammered. "… I saw something."

It just came out. What was I supposed to do, lie?

"What?" he said, now growing nervous as I was. Fuck, why did I do that?

"Th-There was something outside the glass, um…" Then I realized, I hadn't told him the whole truth. "A shark or something. Like, a big shark."

Jackson arched his brow, like he always did when he thought I was crazy.

"Are you pranking me?" he asked, his whole demeanor changing from worried to a perky suspicion.

I was dumbfounded. "Huh?" I said, still in a state of clear panic.

"I thought you loved sharks? Go play with your new friend," he joked.

Without a doubt, the alcohol took the edge off of him from earlier, but he had no idea just how serious I was. Maybe that was a good thing, but right now, I needed both of us to leave this room asap.

I kneeled in front of him, looking him in the eye.

"Listen, I don't wanna be in here right now. I'm getting... claustrophobic," I lied (a terrible one, at that). "Let's just go to one of the lounges and hang out there for a bit where there's no open water outside to look at, okay?"

He still wasn't buying it. I'd be skeptical, too, if I were him. I never expressed fear of any sort in regards to the ocean. Even all the scary creatures he feared that swam in the sea, I took a liking to. But not that thing. Not that thing that waited outside...

"Your acting never fails to impress me, dear-

"Jackson!" I snapped.

He turned straight-faced again. I never snapped at him like that before. He knew I wasn't kidding now.

"You're serious," he said. I nodded.

"Just put on your pants and let's go," I insisted. "I-I'll cover your eyes so you don't have to see out there when we cross the room."

"Okay…"

He got up and started to put his pants on.

"By the way," he started, "Did you hear something a minute ago? Or was it just the movie?"

"Hear what?" I asked, a noticeable unease in my voice.

"Well I don't know, I thought I heard something, like a loud rumbling noise. Thought it came from the movie, but then I was like, there's no way, because-"

MuUUUuuuUUUUUUUuuh

We both felt it rumble down in our feet and up to our rib cage, and stared at each other for a moment. Aware of precisely the same thing now, Jackson whispered under his breath, "Honey… what was that?"

Suddenly, the rumble sounded again, followed by the two of us losing balance on both of our feet as we stumbled. We both struggled to hold on to each other while simultaneously trying to grab onto the wall for support. Jackson managed to clutch one of the beams sitting atop the wall, and his strength alone was enough to hold both of us. I held onto him for dear life as the suite continued violently shaking.

His back was to the window as my arms hooked around him for balance. But I could see ahead that the barricade of pillows we'd put up on the window had now fallen, leaving the glass open for a full display of the outside. And to my confusion, I couldn't see anything beyond it. It wasn't a dark blue or black tint this time, but instead, a bright yellowish shade that now covered the window.

The rumbling had now stopped, and it was quiet as a mouse.

"You okay?" Jackson asked.

I didn't say anything. I was too fixated on the window. Why was it that color? It's like we shifted into a different environment altogether. Like a whole new backdrop.

"What the hell?" I muttered.

"Hmm?"

He turned to what I was perceiving and shared the same confusion. It was a strange sight indeed. Then we saw a black circle shift from nowhere and down into different corners of the yellow-filled circular window. The direction of the circle bounced randomly from corner to corner as if it were a corrupted game of Pong, until finally sitting dead center on the glass, facing us.

I felt a sick sensation in my gut, and Jackson's jaw slowly dropped in terror at the realization of what we were now both seeing. It was an eye – the creature's pupil… and it saw us.

MuUUUuuuUUUUUUUuuh

The sound rumbled the whole area again.

"Go, go!" Jackson shouted, trying to lead us both out of the room, and we did just that.

We'd crossed into the bathroom when the lights cut off. There was darkness again. We were blind to the lack of light as we both tripped into each other, him almost knocking me down completely. I grabbed onto what I could only guess was the sink as Jackson quickly grabbed me to keep me from falling.

"You all right?" he said.

"Yeah."

"What the hell is that thing?!" His voice trembled.

"I don't know!" I cried.

We needed to get ahead into the room and out into the main lobby and let someone know what was going on. But the lamp I'd left on in the bedroom ahead was out, too. Otherwise, there'd be some lighted path for us to distinguish. It was pure darkness. The only faint light, if any, came from the dark hue of the water surrounding us.

I pulled out my phone and turned on the flashlight to lead us.

"C'mon," I demanded.

Jackson followed closely behind with his arms still over me for protection. Though, I'm sure it was more for him than it was for me. I could only imagine…

We raced through the bedroom and for the door in a matter of seconds. But in that time, we caught a glimpse of the outside. It was a nightmare. Just an endless void of murky dark water that appeared to stretch for an eternity. We were two small, meaningless creatures in the center of the vast universe.

When we got to the door, I turned the knob and pulled back without hesitation, as Jackson reached over and helped by yanking it back into the wall, and we both hauled ass out of there. In the corridors, the lights were out as well. No source of illumination anywhere except the faint moonlight protruding the ocean's horizon. Like the suite, the halls were made entirely of glass like a giant walkthrough tube to behold the ocean life exterior.

"Which way is it?" I anxiously asked.

"Here," Jackson said, pointing down to the left corridor.

He and I made our way down the halls, but slowly this time. I supposed it was from a backup generator light, but there was now some visible light projecting from the outside of the glass tube. With the help of that, something else outside caught our eye.

It was indescribable. Countless dark silhouettes of fish. Hundreds of them. The ones that had been gone earlier were now all here for us to see beyond the glass. However, something was wrong.

The way in which they swam didn't align in a fluid horizontal motion. Some of their bodies were positioned diagonally, vertically, and in a strange sense, seemed to be merely floating rather than swimming…

Then the realization hit me. They weren't swimming at all. They were dead. Lifelessly drifting in the water down to us.

"Jesus," Jackson gasped.

"L-let's just keep moving," I said, trying to be brave.

Then to our left, the only visible ray of light rose by itself, and shortly after the creature emerged from below, its massive tentacles and fins rising into view, its bright yellow eyes glaring into us. My God, the source of the light was from the damn thing itself. Like an angler fish, it was capable of luminescence to attract its prey, emitting from its fins and tentacles. The hall began to shake as the earth-shattering rumble sounded throughout the structure.

Without hesitation, the two of us raced down the hall to reach the next corridor that would eventually get us to the lobby. We just needed to make it. Where that thing could no longer see us.

All throughout the long glass tube, it followed from the outside in an unsettlingly forbearing nature, as if it knew its place in the animal kingdom hierarchy. We were no challenge for it. It wanted to taunt us. It knew…

We'd managed to run down to the lobby and thankfully, one of the clerks was still there at the counter, likely the one I'd spoken to earlier on the phone. The woman saw us in our state of panic and immediately stood up to ask what was the matter. We told her of the creature that was terrorizing us, to which she was understandably struck by. We even told her about the fish we'd seen that were now regurgitated from the monster. It was hard to say if she bought our story or not, but based on her facial expressions, she innately knew we were dead serious.

The two of us refused to spend another night in that room. We asked if there were any other rooms available that didn't involve windows of any sort, or better yet, any that were at the surface, but truly, Jackson and I both wanted to get the hell out of this place.

A couple of hotel staff offered to take our belongings out of the room and personally hand them over to us in the main lobby, as the clerk informed us that there was a vacancy in the only other room available at the top above the water, on top of the fact that neither one of us agreed to enter that hellish fishbowl again.

•••

In our new more relaxing suite on the surface of the land, it'd taken a while for either one of us to fall back asleep. Jackson, in the shock of it all and for good reason, had taken it harder than me. I lied there with him in bed and stayed until he felt comfortable to drift off.

At some point in the night, I'd got up to peer out the window, which gave a view of the ocean's horizon under the full moon. Any other day, I'd find the sight to be an ethereal beauty, not one to literally die for. What was supposed to have been a beautiful day for the two of us, at the expense of Jackson going out of his way to try and make me happy, was now ruined by the untethered force of nature that resided beneath.

I began to quietly sob, as not to wake Jackson from his slumber, my vision becoming blurred from the muddiness of tears.

But as I looked down again at the ocean below, I could sense that somewhere in my line of sight, it waited. And with a startling revelation that haunted me from when we first laid eyes upon the creature, an undeniable fact rang true. It was fully aware and perceptive of everything around it. Every ounce of fear and every moment of uncertainty Jackson and I shared together was on full display for it to see.

It knew.

CATACLYSM

The sky yawned a growing storm, rumbles of thunder so loud I felt the earth rumble from inside here. Looks like my cue to be on my way. I knew I shouldn't get another shot of whiskey - my mind had wandered enough in the passing hours. Where was I headed? Who knows? Who cares? It didn't really matter right now. I just needed to get away…

The bar was brightly lit and decorated with pink and green neon lights on the outside, contrasting with its light golden brown interior hue. It was clear that the hangout stood for decades, but you wouldn't know that by its hospitality and noticeable renovations.

I and only a few other people sat inside (two other older gentlemen chit-chatting at the barstools). I had no clue where I was. Kansas, I was pretty sure, or maybe Oklahoma. Wherever, I was hours and miles apart from where I was supposed to be. Again, none of that mattered.

The bartender, an older man in his middle ages, came over to me from the other side of the bar.

"Probably best you start hittin' the road, son," he spoke in a smoky but chipper voice. "Looks like a storm's comin' any minute now, and around here, that typically turns into something much worse."

"What's that?" I asked.

"Tornado," he said. "It's that time of the year. I'm guessing you're not from around these parts?"

I smiled bashfully. "You guessed right."

"Well, no harm in that. I'd be more than happy with you staying here, but I gotta start closin' up here soon myself. I've got babies to take care of," – he gives a so-so hand gesture – "Eh, they're getting about close to your age, I should say."

I nodded.

"How old are you, twenty?" he guessed.

"Close," I said. "Twenty-one."

"Ah, about close to what I figured," he nodded. "You in school?"

"Yeah…"

"You like it?"

I shrugged. "If my grades say anything, I guess not."

The man nodded with understanding.

"I never did it myself, just worked," he added. "For some of us, that's all we need."

I looked at my phone and saw that I had two missed calls and unread messages from Seth, my buddy from campus. I rolled my eyes. We were good friends... *were* good friends, as of 17 hours ago. Good laughs, trips, deep conversations, secrets, inside jokes, exchanges of advice... all ruined in a matter of moments in an exchange of heartless, callous words to one another. Currently, I read the messages, asking where I was and to call him, and a voice message I didn't bother to listen to. With a few swift taps, I blocked him.

I stepped out of the bar and looked out at the distant field. There were a few other small buildings in sight - a small convenience store and gas pump - but I was dead smack in the middle of the rural Midwest. Fields of grass and occasionally corn for miles. The sky was turning a dull dismal green, puffy clouds forming above in an unusual shape clumping next to one another. The bartender was right. It was about to get ugly.

•••

I got on the interstate and kept heading north. I swear it'd been damn near 20 minutes ago since I'd passed an exit. I was on the country's longest highway, it seemed, a long line of concrete that stretched for eternity, nothing but endless fields of grass at my sides. As a kid, those were the worst road trips with nothing interesting to look at for hours. Years later, that hasn't really changed.

In the short amount of time from when I left the bar to getting back on the interstate, the sky darkened to damn near pitch black. I couldn't see a thing beyond the vision of my headlights and the occasional cars or trucks that passed by on the opposite lane, as well as a few dazzling but ominous flashes of lightning hidden beyond the clouds.

I turned on the radio to play some music, but at the moment, the local station was giving out a tornado warning that was imminent in the area, telling everyone to take shelter immediately.
The AI-prompted voice from the broadcasting system delivered a foreboding message caught some seconds in:

"...National Weather Service in McPherson has issued a tornado warning for: McPherson County, Kansas, south central Saline County, Kansas, until 11:47 P.M. Central Standard time, at 11:10 P.M. Central Standard time. National Weather Service Doppler radar indicated a severe thunderstorm capable of producing a tornado. This dangerous storm was located... "

In a low subtle tone, I heard what I could only describe as the faint howling of the wind, tuning out the broadcast as background noise. To be sure, I turned down the radio and listened carefully. I heard just fine. It was a faint whistle of wind. It had been so quiet a moment ago - up to this point, matter of fact. Was it really that windy outside? Guess so.

With a crack of lightning and thunder illuminating the darkened sky, it was there that I saw it perched in the distant field on my right. The silhouette of a towering funnel-shaped cloud, a towering giant of rotating wind nearly as black as the wind surrounding it. No way... was that really it?

I wished to do a double-take, but just like that, the flash was brief, and the tornado vanished from my sight, the sky shrouded in darkness once more. If I hadn't blinked for just another millisecond, I may have been certain-

Another flash lit up the sky, and my suspicions were confirmed. Goodness, it was huge! I'd never seen anything like it before. Maybe on TV and in movies and pictures, but never in person. It was astronomically indifferent to its surroundings in both scale and presence, a relentless force of nature, just waiting in the darkness in silence. It was unreal… and unnerving.

The silhouette of the vortex was gone from my sight again once the lightning ceased, but at least I was well aware of its position. It was difficult to say exactly how far it was, but it was a good distance apart from me, at least for now. Again, like a steady rhythm of a tune, the lightning illuminated the darkness, and when I shifted my eyes to take another glance at the twister, I was in disbelief.

It was gone. The damn thing was nowhere in sight. I knew I wasn't crazy. It was just there. I couldn't be seeing things… how did it just-

Suddenly, a bright flash of lightning lit up the sky once more, revealing the colossal whirlwind of a monster, just to the side of the shoulder on the interstate - right next to me.

74

I'd felt fear many times before, but not like this. Not like this…

I was at the mercy of something I had no hope of subduing if my life depended on it. In those next moments, I'd forgotten about my physical body, as my soul already left and my life flashed before me, and the next thing I knew, my car swerved to the opposite side of the road. Seems I hit the brakes right then and there. My instincts decided for me that it was too late. It caught me. I'd have to accept my fate…

But as I regained composure, feeling my hands tightly gripped on the wheel, my foot pressed so hard onto the brake pedal I felt I could snap it, my heartbeat skyrocketing, there was silence. Dead air. Nothing.

Sitting in my car parked perpendicularly in the middle of the road, I turned my head every which way and didn't spot a twister in sight. Baffled wasn't even enough to describe - utterly *stupefied* was more suitable. Where was the roar of the vortex or the gust of wind? It's as if it never existed.

Soon after, another car pulled to the side of the road from behind, their brights blinding me, and the driver stepped out and walked a good distance my way.

"Are you okay?" the passerby asked.

I was still in shock, I could barely speak properly. "D-d-did you see it?" I stammered, pointing my finger towards the direction where I last saw the colossus.

"See what?" they asked.

"The tornado. I-It was right there. Right on the side of the road."

They were perplexed, as they looked to where I was pointing, another brief flash of lightning illuminating the area, showing nothing but more endless fields of grass ahead. They faced me again.

"Are you sure?" they said. "There's nothing there."

I was at a loss for words. Dammit, it was right there. I know it was. How could it vanish and be out of sight so swiftly? A giant swirling mountain of gust? Impossible!

"I mean, there could be," the driver spoke. "It's best if you keep heading towards the nearest exit to find shelter. There's tornado warnings a couple miles ahead of us - 'ahead of us' as in towards Saline. Best to stay clear of that whole area for now. Might get real bad from what my folks are saying." He looked at me, seeing how noticeably petrified I was. "You good, pal?"

I looked at him. What could I say? That he was wrong? He proved otherwise.

I nodded. "Yeah. Thanks. I'm probably just getting tired is all."

He nodded. "Stay safe, man. Probably a good idea to, you know, get out the middle of the road."

"Yeah," I chuckled.
He got back into his car and drove back down the interstate, and I soon did the same.

•••

Still had 5 more miles to go before I'd make it to the nearest exit. That's all I needed. Then I could finally get the fuck off of this road. I just needed a recharge. An energy drink maybe. No, what I really needed was rest. I knew that much. But the nearest motel was still some ways ahead, about another 28 miles.

I heard a light tap on my windshield, then another, then several at the same time, until finally I saw the tiny drops of rain hitting my windshield. I smacked my mouth. Of all times it chooses to rain, now? In a matter of seconds, light rain turned into heavy rain, forcing me to adjust my wipers to the highest setting. It was a struggle to keep my eyes fixed on the road through the blurred glass as they wig-wagged left and right.

Crackles of thunder boomed through the night. The storm wasn't letting up anytime soon. It had a point to be made. But even through the boisterous sound, I could still hear a faint howl of wind, like the one I heard moments before…

It was so low, yet so resonant, gradually protruding my ears, almost like the hum of a creature.
In the blink of an eye, the area flashed a bright purple hue from bolts of lightning, revealing the shape of the vortex in the distance, now on my left. The lightning bolts ceased, blinding me to its presence again. I'd have to wait for the lightning to reveal its location.

"What the hell?" I said to myself. I couldn't believe it.

Another cluster of lightning sparked, and I saw the shape again, but I could swear it was getting closer. Again, the clusters ceased, and it was gone in a flash. Once more, this repeated, confirming my beliefs that the twister was indeed edging closer to the freeway, directly in my path. How could it be doing that? How was it keeping up with me so fast - so precisely?!

I pressed on the gas, speeding down the wet highway as all get-out. It was dangerous, yes, but as was the twister. There was no time to consider the risks right now. There's no way I wouldn't be able to outrun this thing by hitting 65, or even 70 miles per hour.

Another flash showed the twister gaining on me, moving dangerously fast and close to the edge. It's as though it were matching my speed. It was keeping up with me all the way, like it was intentionally chasing me. Like it had a mind of its own. The lightning flashed again, the twister now just several yards away from the shoulder. I looked at the speedometer, the needle sliding into 90 mph now, slipping into 95.

"C'mon, c'mon," I uttered through clenched teeth.

I was about to hit 100 any second now. Geez, I never had any business driving this fast ever, but there was a first for everything. The crackling sound of thunder began to hover over me, and I knew what would inevitably follow. It would be right there. It was going to get me…

I'd hit a slight bump in the road, and my car began to swerve diagonally along the pavement. Fuck, I was beginning to skid. I straightened out the car with the alignment of the road, only to have the same result in the opposite direction. I was hydroplaning in the middle of a thunderstorm and a tornado right on my ass. The car lost all control, and as it skidded towards the road off into the side, I closed my eyes. This was it...

The bright flash of lightning followed, lighting up the night sky in a spectacular display of purple electric tree roots. I went off the road and into a field of grass, the vehicle coming to a brutal halt. I experienced whiplash as my neck jerked violently to the side. I couldn't feel the pain at the moment, however. I was still hooked on adrenaline.

As I sat in the car waiting for my inevitable demise, I noticed that odd sensation as with before when I stopped myself in the middle of the road.

Silence.

I leaned my head forward, peering under the windshield, searching for the monster. Nothing. Nowhere in sight. I stepped out of the car in the middle of the grassy field, glancing every which way, only to find thunder and lightning hidden under the dark clouds. And another thing I just noticed, was that the rain was gone as well.

•••

Once I'd made it to the exit, I got off the highway and pulled into a gas station so I could grab a quick energy drink and maybe a snack or two. I was a bit tired but not *that* tired. I know what I saw. I don't ever hallucinate like that. I don't do drugs, LSD, nothing of the sort. I didn't imagine it. I couldn't have.

I'd gotten a call from Trish, one of my friends in our group, Seth included. I wondered if Seth asked her to speak to me, or if she was doing this out of the genuine interest of a friend. I'd hope for the latter. Trish had a good heart and only wanted peace between us and everyone around her.

"Hey," she said on the other end.

"Hey," I shyly answered.

"How's it goin'?"

"I think you already know."

"Well... yeah, Seth did tell me what happened. But I didn't call because of him. I'm just worried, is all."

From my car, I gazed out into the ghastly black sky, the gas station the only source of illumination for miles in a twenty-foot radius, as though I were sitting at the edge of the universe.

"I know," I assured her. "I'm fine. As for Seth... well, not really my problem."

"C'mon, I want you two to work this out."

I shook my head. "No. He crossed the line. I'm not interested in this whole 'I'm sorry, I shouldn't have said so-and-so' crap. No, screw that."

She sighed on the other end.

"I'm not against your side, by the way," she remarked. "I think he was definitely in the wrong, but..."

"What? You agree with him?"

"Well, you did say your grades aren't exactly... stellar."

"They're not. That's my business, though."

"It is. But I don't think his intentions were truly bad. I think he's just worried. I am, too."

I chuckled sarcastically. "If I wanted to be lectured by my parents, I would've just moved back in with them. I decide when it's time to throw the towel in."

"Look, my sister used to struggle for a while in school. Very smart, very bright just like everyone else in her class. And after a few doctor's appointments we got her the medication she needed and she was right back on track. It wasn't a crutch; it wasn't a handicap. It's just... a different challenge she had to deal with. It didn't make her any 'less than' than anyone else."

"That's great, Trish. And I'm happy for your sister. But that's got nothing to do with me."

There was a moment of awkward silence between us. I'd never been so aggressive towards her before, and I'm sure she didn't know how to react. I felt bad for raising my voice at her, but my point still stood. That's what I believed, anyways.

"Where are you?" she asked. "I knocked on your door earlier, but you weren't there. Derrick said you weren't in class either."

I swallowed timidly. "Somewhere," I answered. "Miles away from campus."

"Please come home. You don't even need to go right back to class, but just please, I want you back here. I want to fix this, even if you don't. Even if it's not my problem. I just…"

She wasn't wrong, I didn't want to fix it. Not now, though. Right now, I wanted to run.
I hung up the phone.

•••

While I was in the store, I emptied my bladder (since I didn't shit my pants enough earlier from the whole ordeal) and grabbed two Red Bulls and two roller bites. As I was checking out with the cashier, the lights began to flicker until they eventually shut off entirely.

"Great," the clerk uttered.

This storm was no joke. The power line was likely hit. The clerk fumbled with the register trying to get it to work, but it also was having issues reading my card.

"Sorry, just a moment," they said, as they handed me back my card and stepped from the counter and into the back, probably to activate a backup generator.

I leaned on the counter as I waited. It was still and inaudible until I heard the faint whistle of wind from outside. The same as before when I was on the road. I slowly stepped toward the large windows to take a look outside. It was dark both in and out of the gas station. Not so much as the faint glimmer of moonlight seemed prevalent in the night sky. Only thing was the outside fluorescent lights at the pumps. They were enough, if not a lot to make up for the lack of visibility. Standing there looking into the black abyss of the night sky in the field ahead, an unsettling sensation itched me, as if wherever I was currently staring, something was staring back…

I stepped outside, standing by my car in the parking lot, keeping my eyes fixated on the black void of space. I didn't blink for one second, as if doing so would be the difference between life or death…

Something inside me knew…

A burning sensation at the side of my temples, an electric charge of static rushing through me…

My eyes had nowhere else to lock on, and no intentions of looking elsewhere…

And then there it was.

Creeping more and more into the frame of light emitting from the pumps, the behemoth emerged from the shadows in a circling wall of wind. And as with before, what was most unsettling was not only its sheer size and how close it was at this very moment. It was how noiseless it appeared. How it snuck up on me with no sign or warning. It was almost as silent as a predator in the night. I couldn't exactly hear the roar of the beast, but instead *felt* it. The mass and ferocity of the monster shook me at my core, a strong vibration oscillating through my chest and down to my knees through the ground. It's as if it… *followed* me.

I quickly got in my car and sped the hell out of there, heading in the opposite direction down the highway, pressing my foot hard on the gas. I had to have hit 100 mph or more. If there was ever a more appropriate time to speed, this was it.

I hadn't bothered looking back. Five, maybe seven minutes passed before the rush of adrenaline finally died down, and I slowly began to hit the brakes, bringing the car to a gradual stop. I took deep steady breaths, regaining my composure. What was I thinking? I looked in the rearview mirror, able to see the faint light of the gas station behind in the distance. I stepped out of the car and stood by to take a better look. The distant lightning and thunder rumbled together, a spectacular instrument sounding throughout the night sky, showcasing the tornado in all its glory. It was captivating to look at from such a safe distance, yet likewise terrifyingly beautiful. A force of nature unlike any other.

But I knew, it wasn't real. And as before, it was merely a facade - a trick of the mind. I don't know if I was ridiculously that tired or what, and the stress certainly didn't help either, but-
The lights of the gas station began dimming in the distance as the towering titan engulfed it in darkness, tearing the structure apart to bits in a matter of seconds. I watched in horror at its sheer power. The clerk was still in there. That poor man...

"God..." I uttered.

It was real. The goddamn thing was real.

Then, a stroke of wind tickled the back of my neck, like the brush of a hand, and goosebumps trailed throughout my body. My skin grew stone-cold with dread. The howl of wind returned, but from multiple directions this time. From my left, right, behind me - everywhere.

I turned to face behind me, staring at the pitch-black wall of night. I could hear the thunder rumbling trailing through the clouds, its growl growing closer and closer to where I stood. And strangely, for a moment, there was pure stillness. Dead silence, as though the world around me came to a standstill.

I stood in darkness on the side of the road, turning to face the twister in the distance, but it was nowhere in sight. In the blink of an eye, it disappeared.

Suddenly, a blinding flash of lightning, followed by a deafening roar of thunder, revealed three monstrous tornadoes surrounding me in all directions. I was cornered. There was nowhere to run.
As I looked up at the towering titans, I got down on my knees, raising my arms to shield my face, feeling smaller than I ever have. I was an ant to them. Meaningless. Kneeling to such power fitting for a god - or whatever deity had dominion over this land and universe - was only appropriate. At this moment, I'd die the worst possible way imagined.

In *fear*.

No. I couldn't.

I ran to the side of the interstate, watching as the
funnels began to close in on me, and scanned for an
overpass. There was the one across from me that I'd
driven under when I took that exit, but that was
much too far for me to reach at this rate. I can't
outrun a twister, let alone three.
Instinct overtook me again, similar to the first run-in
I'd had. My body began to act, as there was no time
to stand around and think. Whatever split decision I
was going to choose at this very moment had better
be the right one.

I jumped down and rolled into the ditch at the side
of the road and huddled in a ball position, covering
my head and neck. I felt so defenseless and
powerless. But this was the best I could do.
The rumbles and belting of the twisters drew closer,
akin to the roar of a jet blast or rocket. It was the
loudest sound I'd ever heard. It drowned out
everything else. I clasped my hands against my ears,
risking any protection from my head, as the noise
was too overbearing. Even still, it was too much to
handle.

The high-speed winds passed atop me and the ditch,
leaving me unscathed. The twisters were without a
doubt nearly above me now, if not about to pass this

way. Several feet ahead of me, my car slammed violently into the ditch, shattering every window and smashing every metal into a large dent.

I screamed at the top of my lungs, though, it was useless and mute against the overpowering roar of the titans. In my head, I remember praying that it would all be over soon…

And just as quickly and vigorously as it began, it was suddenly over. The deafening roar began to die off, the winds gradually slowed to a light breeze and eventually ceased altogether. It was a once-in-a-lifetime phenomenon to witness, especially in the aftermath, so calm and serene, so quiet and tranquil, as if nothing ever happened.

I didn't move at first. I refused to leave the ditch for a long period, uncertain if each of them was gone. I knew the twisters subsided, yet I lay there for minutes - *hours* for all I know. My sense of time and relativity to the cataclysm felt nonexistent. The whole thing lasted maybe five minutes tops. It felt so much longer than that.

I finally got up and pulled myself out of the ditch. I took a glance at my car again. It was totaled. I could either stay here and hope to catch a ride from a good samaritan or get to stepping. After what I'd just been through, I'd take anything, including walking for miles upon end rather than relieve that nightmare once more.

•••

I disconnected my mind and body from one another to keep pushing forward. I had to keep going. I trudged for maybe an hour (or as I assumed before, might've been longer) before I heard the whistling again. I halted in my tracks, turning my head to the side, staring into the abyss beyond a large cornfield. I stood there and faced the sky wall, waiting. I knew it was there. It was waiting. There were no nearby ditches, no forms of shelter in sight. This was it.

The low audible rumble gradually increased. It was getting closer. Only a matter of time…

A flash of bright light began to drown me, not from lightning, however, but something else entirely. The rumble was now directly across from me on the road, and I turned to face two giant headlights charging at full speed, accompanied by the blaring horn of a semi-truck.

I dove into the shoulder of the highway, barely avoiding being pulverized. The roar of the semi passed, like the bellow of a monster of its own. I laid there on the ground again, rattled by the last of many close calls tonight.

Some ways ahead, the trucker brought the 18-wheeler to a full stop, pulling into the shoulder as much as possible. They stepped out of the truck and began to approach me.

"Are you all right? Hello?" the man called into the night.

Like before, I was unable to move. I trembled uncontrollably.

"Hello?" the trucker called again.

For the life of me, I couldn't speak either. There was a lump in my throat to where I couldn't utter a single syllable. The trucker pulled out a flashlight, the beam of light pointed above me, and the man began jogging towards me. I could tell he was out of shape by the width of his waist and the way he hurried. But when he finally did make it over to me, the light was now beaming directly on my face, irritating my pupils, forcing me to squint.

"Sir, you okay?" the man worriedly asked.

I slowly stood up to face him, still unable to muster any words. My throat was still restricted. However, one noise did utter from my mouth, with a constrained effort. It was a sob.

♦♦♦

I sat in the passenger seat of the semi next to the man. He was in his late to early forties, guessing by a glance. I didn't ask either. What I knew for certain was that he was kind. He offered to take me to the nearest roadside motel. At least there I'd be able to rest and figure out what I would do from there in the morning.

"I thought for sure I'd hit you," the man said, sounding relieved. "What are you doing out here? There's tornado warnings, you know?"

He saw that I was still visibly shaken, and I still had a hard time speaking. He didn't pry too much, seeming to understand. Even if I told him, would he?

"You seem like a young guy," he talked some more. "You got any family?" I nodded. "Got a car?"

"I did," I answered. It almost sounded funny coming out of my mouth.

"I won't ask too many personal questions, don't worry. Just curious, is all. I don't have much of a family myself. Just a daughter. She's my world, as far as I'm concerned. She's around your age if I could guess yours. How old are you?"

That question again? "Twenty-one," I answered.

The man chuckled. "Yeah, that's about right," he said. "Still young, but old enough to do what you want, yeah?" I shrugged. "Look, I know it's none of my business, but whatever you're going through at this moment now in your life, it's only temporary. Like a bad storm - it dies eventually."

"How do you know?" I retorted.

"Because I've lived. We're all different. Got different experiences, of course. Not always the best role models, not always the best people around you with your best interests in mind. But... I know through the wreckage, through pain, there's always a way out. We don't have to stay where things make us feel less than. Or you can do like some people and stay and fight, grow stronger. But you might be missing out on a ton of other things you could've done. It's up to us."

At the time I didn't think much of what the man was lecturing me about. But looking back on it, it's exactly what I needed to hear.

We'd made it to a roadside motel and I thanked the man for not only the ride, but for saving my life. He was humble, not thinking much of it, but of course, I didn't tell him about what I'd endured. As he said, we're all different in our walks of life, and it didn't matter to him.

I checked in a room for myself with nothing but my phone and the clothes on my back. My phone battery was at ten percent, and I didn't have a charger on me. I stared and watched as the number dropped to nine, periodically checking on it, then watching it change to eight.

I sighed. I kept hesitating. I was exhausted and could pass out at any minute, but knew that if I did, I wouldn't have a working phone in the morning.

I immediately went to my contacts and tapped 'call' to the person I needed right now the most. I waited as it rang, hearing my own heart thump between my ears with anticipation. Would he even answer?

Then, a voice came on the other end.

"Hello?" they answered.

"Hey Dad," I responded.

"Hey. What's up?"

"Um… I'm at a motel in Kansas. I don't know exactly where but… can you please come get me? My car's ruined. I don't have anywhere to go."

"Kansas? What're you doing there? Don't you have school?"

"Yeah… about that… I don't think it's for me."

Brief silence. I was waiting for the lecture, but it never came.

"Send me the address, okay?" my father said.

"Thank you," I said, a tear rolling down my face.

"Don't go anywhere, okay? I'm on my way now."

"Okay."

"I love you."

"Love you, too."

The line disconnected.

I used the last bit of battery that I had on my phone and sent my current location to him. After I did so, I collapsed onto the soft bed, not bothering to take off my clothes or shoes, and finally drifted to sleep.

SEDONA

Road trips were always fun, even if I didn't get to go on a lot of them. I was invited to tag along for a visit to Sedona, Arizona, along with three other people - my younger sister Janice (19), Kenneth (25), and Matt (27). I was 23-years-old and a recent college graduate. For now, there was a little free time while I applied and waited to hear back from several employers.

Kenneth and Matt were doing this for their new 'horror' podcast, where they covered a variety of creepy, unexplained stories and phenomena around the world. Typical things you'd expect from an amateur horror podcaster. Several of the listeners recommended they cover the topic of certain 'hot spots' or zones that seem to harbor paranormal and downright strange activity. So, to suffice, they decided to pay the city of Sedona a visit themselves, since they were adventurous like that.

The area had a reputation for being what's known as a 'spiritual vortex,' a zone where people seem to be at a sense of peace, calming, and thought to bring healing capabilities to whoever stands in it long enough.

So why use it as the topic of a horror podcast? Well, it's also known to be the sightings of many UFOs and other paranormal events from time to time that can't quite be explained. Supposedly, there are other 'zones' like this in the world. Skinwalker Ranch in Utah. Taos, New Mexico. Aokigahara forest in Japan. The Bermuda Triangle. They all have the same thing in common.

Energy. Lots of peculiar energy compared to the rest of the world. Matt and Kenneth, being the urban explorers that they were, wanted to nosedive right into the heart of Sedona's vortexes. The main one we planned on hitting first was Bell Rock, a large butte with one helluva peak that gives a panoramic view to die for.

Usually, I'd say fuck no to things like this, but then Janice agreed to tag along. As a matter of fact, she agreed without hesitation, as she was more adventurous than I was, always getting into things, in both a good and bad way. She also got into more trouble than I did. It was just me and her growing up, and one could imagine how much blame I'd get for when something unfortunate would happen to her. She was 100-percent on board, and even wanted to hike some of the trails with the two guys while she insisted I could stay in the van if I wanted.

Nope.

I knew Kenneth and Matt well enough to assume they were good people, truly, but older sibling instincts refused to let her go by herself with two older men. Even if I was overthinking it, that just wasn't something I could afford to risk.

•••

I knew of van dwellers and people who'd put a lot of effort into making their home on wheels look and feel like an actual home, but damn, Matt and Kenneth weren't playing around. It was a high-top conversion van, owned by Matt, with more room than you'd expect from the outside looking in.

They fit a couch, beanbag, tabletop and chair, computer, mini-fridge, sink, mini-oven, and stovetop all in such a compact yet roomy living space. It was also decorated with various stickers and posters, and the floral pattern curtains paired nicely with the brown wooden interior of the walls.

What really set the mood, though, were the strands of LED lights taped around the corners and along the walls, each circuit lit in a combination of colors ranging from red, blue, green, and yellow, making it look like Christmas.

Janice and I were inside the back, sorting through our things and getting settled in.

"I'm glad you decided to come along," she mentioned.

"What, you thought I was just gonna let you go by yourself?" I remarked.

"You know I'm an adult now, right?"

"Yes, and you're still naive."

She rolled her eyes at me.

"Think about it, me leaving you with two grown men?" I added.

"Um, have you seen the two of them?" Janice retorted. "Like, I'm just saying, I think even *you* could take them by yourself. Hell, even Mama could."

"That's because Mama can actually fight."

"I can fight," she argued, sounding offended.

"Eh, you talk a good talk."

She scoffed. "Whatever, you know I can scrap when I need to."

"Suuure."

She hit me on the shoulder, as I teasingly smiled.

Then Kenneth came into the back where we were.

"Got everything?" he asked both of us.

"Yeah, think so," Janice said.

"Sorry there's not another bed for you to sleep in, Joe," he said to me.

"Oh that's okay, Janice will be perfectly fine on the beanbag in the corner," I dryly humored.

"Ha-ha," she remarked.

In one hand, Kenneth held two walkie-talkies by their antennas and raised them.

"Brought some two-way radios, just 'cause," said. "In case we feel like playing around or testing other points at the summit and other spots."

"Ooh, sounds fun," Janice sounded pleased. She then took note of the thing in his other hand. "What's that?"

"Oh, this?" Kenneth said, raising the device for us to see.

It was a small wooden contraption in the shape of a triangle and what looked like a gemstone tied to the end of a string.

"It's a pendulum," he noted.

"What's it for?" she asked.

He then walked over to the tabletop and placed the pendulum on its legs to stand freely, as the gemstone now began to swivel left and right on a single axis from the string.

"Well," he started, "They say when you're near a site that's full of paranormal or high amounts of energy, the pendulum's supposed to swing nearer in that direction or whatever."

"Who's *they*?" Janice remarked.

Kenneth looked at her then shrugged. "I don't know," he said frankly.

Janice laughed amusedly.

"Apparently, that's what it does," Kenneth went on.

"What kind of rock is that?" she pointed.

"Oh, that's amethyst. Supposedly it wards off bad spirits, so, you know, probably a good idea to have it around while we're camping out there."

"I thought the vortexes harbor good energy only?"

"They do, but, you never know."

You never know...

"Oh that's okay," Janice said as she clasped her hands on my shoulder. "Joe here will protect us, because our grandmother said he's *special*," she said in a mocking tone and a big smile.

Janice then walked out of the van.

"O... kay," Kenneth replied.

But I knew exactly what she was referring to.

•••

We made a rest stop at a gas station seemingly in the middle of nowhere. No big-name shop like Shell or Texaco, but a compact blue wooden exterior structure with two gas pumps that look something straight out of the 70s. They did, however, have a good selection of snacks and drinks on par with a 7-Eleven.

Everyone used the restroom and got something of nourishment at the least. I decided to grab a water and head back to the van before everyone else so that I could light and smoke a cigarette (or 'cancer stick,' as Janice referred to them as). Soon after, Matt followed, while Janice and Kenneth were still in the station looking for something to buy, or probably laughing and bullshitting. Those two, I swear. They shouldn't shut up the whole drive.

Matt and I sat along the edge at the back of the van with the door open. From where we parked, the view of a wide range of mountains and desert terrain was ethereal, something I wasn't used to from North Florida.

"Those two are something, aren't they?" Matt said as he cracked open his Red Bull.

"Hmm," I scoffed, taking a hit of my cigarette.

"He is on the older tip, though, so…"

"I don't care who she sees, if that's what it is," I responded. "Kenneth's all right, I think."

"No bad vibes from him?"

I shook my head. "Nope," then took another hit.

"No bad vibes from me?"

I turned to him and glared into his eyes. The intention was to make him uncomfortable. My humor was dry like that. After a few seconds, I backed off.

"No," I said.

Matt chuckled. "That's good to know," he said.

"At least I don't think so."

"Would you have tagged along if you thought otherwise?"

I shrugged. "Doesn't matter. Janice tagged along, so I did."

"And if she didn't?"

"If she didn't what?"

"If she didn't decide to come along, would you have still?"

I took another hit from my cigarette, taking in and exhaling the menthol, thinking of how nicely to put this.

"Honestly, probably not," I answered. It was really *definitely* not, but I didn't want to hurt his feelings.

"At least you're honest," Matt noted.

I shook my head. "It's nothing against you or Kenneth or your guys' podcast. It's just… I don't like to play with energies like that."

Matt furrowed his brow. "Energies?"

I nodded. "The vortex?"

"But it's supposed to be peaceful. You know, a 'positive' energy."

"Yeah, it may be peaceful for some, hell, even most. But for others… you just never know."

Matt paused, tapping his foot on the ground, then took a sip of his drink. After a while, he spoke again.

"Have you had bad experiences before?" he asked.

I looked at him. "No," I answered.

"You believe in… possession? Or being overtaken by another force?"

"I believe in protecting your aura. At all times. Like you would your own life." Matt nodded with content. "My grandmother, before she passed, told me when I was younger that me and a few other people in the family had 'the gift.'"

"The gift?" Matt said.

"Like a… not necessarily psychic or anything like that, but that me and the others were just more… sensitive to certain energies. *Vibrational* frequencies, they say." I shrugged. "I don't know how true it all actually is, though. I don't believe in

109

absolutes. Angels, demons, gods, divine intervention. But that grey area always tests my faith every now and then…"

Then I saw the look in Matt's eyes. Maybe he was wary or maybe he was regretting me coming along. Wasn't too sure.

"Does Janice have the gift, too?" he asked.

"My grandmother says no," I answered. "Then again, she never seemed to take a liking to Janice, for whatever reason. She seemed to cherish me more. I'm not surprised Janice is the way she is."

"How's that?"

"Just… free-spirited. Unhinged. Spiritual. Into yoga. Trying to find an inner peace and being one with the universe. Stuff like that. I see it as a way of compensating for our grandmother's indifference. Basically a 'fuck you' to her."

"Wow. What do you think might happen if you get near the vortex?" he asked.

I slowly shook my head. "I have no idea."

We hit the road again. About another 4 hours before we'd make it to Bell Rock. Janice and I played cards for a bit, chit-chatted here and there, and Kenneth, Matt, and I rotated between taking turns driving the van.

Eventually, we made it to the first stop, and found a good spot to camp out not too far from Bell Rock, according to Matt. We decided to take a short hike around the area, take some pictures and vlogs, etc.

Sedona is in a league of its own, I thought to myself. It didn't seem quite like the typical American city I was used to. It was akin to stepping on Mars. Rock, sand, mountains, complemented with patches of grass and cacti. It felt like I was in another world entirely.

As we walked, I took note of a tall saguaro cactus surrounded by other shorter cacti and flowers. I told Janice it'd be a nice backdrop for a photo shoot. I had the good camera while she just had her phone.

She stood next to the tall plant - taller than *her* - and she began to strike various silly and some very Instagram-worthy poses.

"I'm ready for my close-up, Mr. Photographer," she played around.

"My, my, madame, you've gotten fat," I teased in a heavy French accent.

"Oh please!"

She really wasn't fat in the slightest, I just liked to mess with her from time to time. She definitely was in better shape than the rest of us. I couldn't knock her for that.

As I snapped various pictures of her, taking different angles, poses, trying to get better lighting, I got down on one knee, pointing the lens at just the right angle, finding the perfect shot.

"That's money right there," I commented.

"Well shit, watcha waitin' for?" Janice exclaimed, holding her smile.

But before I could snap the photo, a loud ringing noise emerged in both of my ears. It crescendoed, then lowered, then raised in volume again, a pulsating sort of sensation. Regardless, the sound was distracting and unusual. Were my ears ringing? Probably, but they never rang like this.

"Joe?" Janice said impatiently.

I lowered the camera, where she could now see my face was disgruntled.

"You okay?" she asked, concerned.

I stood up. "Do you hear that?" I said.

"Hear what?"

"That sound. That ringing."

She looked puzzled. "No…"

I turned my head in every which way across the desert, unsure of what I would even be looking for until suddenly, it stopped. The ringing was gone, and it fell silent. Only thing I could hear was the slight breeze of wind.

"Are you fucking with me?" she said.

"What? No, why would I be?" I said, seriously. I messed with her a lot, but not like that. Never pranked her once in her entire life.

She chuckled and walked past me to catch up with the other two, patting me on the shoulder as she did so. "Never mind, 'gifted one.'"

I stood there for a moment. I didn't understand what the heck just happened, but decided to brush it off and keep on moving down the trail.

•••

I don't remember how long I'd been asleep, but I woke up and found myself alone in the van. It was nighttime outside. Worried, I quickly got up and looked outside the window to check and see if maybe they were in the front.

Nobody.

I went out and saw that we were parked atop a sandy hill. They'd set up a small camp of some sort with three pull-out chairs and a large mat laid flat, which I already knew was Janice's yoga mat. In the distance, I saw the three of them down about 23 yards away walking towards a mountain top. Could that be it? The vortex? I thought I told this chick not to leave without me, especially once they started the hike.

I saw Janice turn back to look, and she noticed me.

"Joe!" she called to me. I shook my head. "Come on! We're gonna take some videos of the vortex!"

I thought about it. Really thought about it. At this point, I just decided F it. Something told me that she'd be all right. After my many objections to Janice going by herself with the two, finally, my intuition spoke to me. My gut never lies, so I knew I could trust it. Only this one time, though.

"I'm good," I declined. "Go on without me."

"You sure, bro?" Kenneth asked.

"I'll stay behind and watch the van."

"Ah, no one's gonna steal it."

I cocked my brow. "You sure about that? It's a nice van."

"Nobody's gonna steal that junk."

Matt hit him on the shoulder. "Fuck you," he said, and Kenneth laughed.

I turned and started walking back towards the van.

"Whatever," Janice spoke. "But you're coming to take pictures with me when the sun comes up, ya hear?"

I raised my hand and gave her a firm thumbs up.

I laid on the comfy bed in the van with my noise-canceling headphones over my ears as I listened to music. The inside Christmas lights kept the area illuminated. Through the window, the night sky bathed in stars of various different shapes. I recognized the Sagittarius constellation, just aside from Gemini, but couldn't make out much more from this view.

Abruptly, my ears began to ring again. The same one from before. It grew louder in pitch the more I listened. So loud to the point where I couldn't even hear the music anymore. I removed my headphones and scratched and rubbed against my ears, wincing at the sound. The noise wasn't exactly painful, but grew noticeably more discomforting.

I got up to look around, to see if maybe there was a device inside that might be the source of the noise, but it was hard to tell the direction from which it came. I checked the walkie-talkie to see if that could be it, but pressing it to my ear, I still heard the sound radiating from elsewhere.

I stopped for a moment to listen, and when I did, I realized it wasn't exactly a ring, but more in resemblance to a *hum*. Crossing the line between the stroke of a chord of an instrument... or the audible sound of something else entirely that I couldn't decipher at the moment.

Just as suddenly as the humming initiated, it ceased at once. The van fell silent. Dead silent.

I stepped outside again, finding it unusual that the same volume from within the vehicle matched the desert. Pure silence. It was almost distracting to all five of my senses. My body was confused.

I saw the three of them in the distance still, nearing the vortex, about to reach the edge any minute now to begin their ascent.

I decided to sit in one of the foldout chairs in front of the van and light a 'cancer stick.' I gazed at the night sky where I could now see the full layout of the celestial bodies above. Breathtaking, needless to say. Out here where there were no city lights, the entire display of stars and constellations were there for us to take in. If anything, this was worth the long trip.

The pendulum sat just beyond where myself and the other chairs stood, in place of where I figured a campfire should've been. I was surprised to see that it swiveled just barely left and right.

"Hmm," I laughed internally, taking another drag from my cigarette.

As I sat and smoked, I noticed that not only was there no noise, but likewise, even so much as a tiny breeze was nonexistent. I had no sensation of the air around me, no feel for any particular temperature, neither hot nor cold, dry or damp. It was as if I were sitting in a vacuum. How was the pendulum moving, now that I think about it? Couldn't do that without the wind, right?

I took note of the smoke as I exhaled, following its trail. Bizarrely, the smoke didn't merely dissolve into the air, but shot in a clear pathway upwards in a stream, curving inward in the direction south of me. Yet still, I felt no wind blowing in that direction. No wind whatsoever.

The humming resumed. Thrown off, the hairs on my neck raised at the abrupt return.

I could hear it clearly and audibly as I did in the van like it was right next to me. I looked around again to see if there was any possible direction for the sound to be emitting from again, but it was still very hard to tell. It was so strange.

When I looked down at the pendulum again, I grew wide-eyed.

The crystal stopped swinging entirely, and instead was pulled completely in one direction, suspended in an impossibly still state. I thought my eyes were deceiving me, but I went over and kneeled to get a closer look, and saw that it did seem to be pulled at one clear angle, as though it were attracted to an invisible force - or a magnetic field of sorts.

I turned to face the direction the crystal was, which pointed directly to the van, and was taken aback by the lights inside. They each began to flash in a sequence that made it appear as though they were looping in a complete circle inside - a phi phenomenon. All of the colors - red, blue, yellow, green - alternated and moved down the line of each circuit one by one.

Could they do that? I hadn't played with the settings or seen Matt show us any other sorts of tricks and sequences it could perform. Either way, how could they just do that by themselves? Did he set it from his phone? Impossible, I thought. They were way too far away for the Bluetooth to even work. Even still, it wouldn't make sense for him to do so.

I turned to face the three in the distance again, seeing that they were now starting the climb up the rock. It was right then and there that I noticed something very particular about the structure as a whole. It had twin peaks at the summit, identical in shape, almost like cone pyramids, as the base took the form of a rocky pyramid. There also was hardly anything surrounding the vicinity. No grass, cacti, anything. Only barren desert and rock. Around where we parked and set up our camping site only lie a few remnants of any sort of vegetation. Then I knew...

We weren't at Bell Rock at all. This was the wrong spot.

I looked back down at the pendulum, and to my shock, it was now pointed downwards at full rest. Not even swinging. I turned to face the van and saw that the lights were now completely off. My eyes narrowed. I put out my cigarette, dropping it to the ground and stomping out the bud.

Hopefully at least one of the walkie-talkies Kenneth brought was in the van. I opened the door to the back and entered, shutting it behind me. It was too dark now with the lights off, so I used my phone flashlight to search for it. Bingo, one was sitting on the table, and I grabbed and pressed the push-to-talk button.

"Janice, can you hear me?" I spoke.

I waited a moment for a response. Nothing. I pressed it again.

"Janice, can you hear me?" I said loudly and clearly.

A few moments passed. Then her voice sounded from the other end, readable but very staticky.

"*What's up, chickenbutt?*" she said back.

I rolled my eyes. "Hey, I don't think we're at the right spot."

"*Whatcha mean?*"

"I *mean*, I don't think this is Bell Rock."

"*Why do you say that?*"

"Just look at the peak. It's nothing like it. It's not even shaped like it."

"But Joe, I feel it. Like, we haven't even reached the top yet, but I swear, I feel its energy, Joe. It's real. It's... it's alive. It's beautiful."

I'm sure there was no doubt about it. I'm glad that whatever energy she was taking in felt good on her end, but whatever energy that began to overtake what now surrounded the campsite didn't match hers. It felt wrong. I knew something wasn't right. Something felt off...

"We've been climbing and... so f... ar it's... been... ve... er... y..."

She was breaking up badly, as more static overpowered her transmission. Were they too far? I don't know, but the reach should've been well within good range from where we were from each other.

"Janice?" I transmitted.

No answer.

Screw this. I reached for my phone in my pocket and decided to just call her instead. I waited as it dialed, putting the phone on speaker. Lo and behold, I heard her phone ring from inside the van. She left it behind.

"Fucking idiot," I muttered.

I hung up the phone and dialed for Matt, when suddenly another transmission came through the radio.

It wasn't Janice's voice.

Under a heavy load of static, the hum faintly emerged.

In the corner of my eye, further from me towards the sink, a single red Christmas light remained on. It was the only thing illuminated inside the van. Then it shut off, but was quickly replaced by the red bult next to it, giving the illusion that the light was moving. It followed on in the same pattern, inching closer towards my direction, as though it had a life of its own. As the red light inched over, the hum grew more and more resonant, feeling closer.

The single red orb trailed down the string of circuits until eventually, it was right across from me from where I stood. The light remained for a moment, burning brightly as I locked eyes on it, as though we were in a staring match.

And just like that, the humming ceased again, and the light suddenly died, fading to black.

In the blink of an eye, red lights filled every circuit along the van, a crimson luminescence engulfing the interior around me. Startled, I quickly tried to push the button again to call the others, but a loud error beep kept emitting along with a red light on the radio, letting me know that someone else was currently using the channel. I heard nothing, though.

Then the lights rapidly strobed in quick bursts of terrifyingly disorienting red flashes, as the humming returned louder than before, like the unified chant of hundreds of people around me.

Panicked now, I darted out of there and stood at the edge of the hill, waving my arms to get the three's attention.

"Janice!" I called.

Curious, I looked at the pendulum again, seeing that it was now swaying side-to-side in a frantic motion, going haywire.

I glanced at the three turning back to face my direction. I doubt we'd be able to hear exactly what the other was saying. From what I could make out,

Janice pulled out her binoculars. As she did so, I began motioning with hand signals for them to call it off.

I then jumped at the sound of Janice's bloodcurdling scream across the distance.

I turned to the van. The red lights continued to emit for a moment, only for all but two of them to remain. From where I stood, they were positioned in a way that looked as though it were two glaring eyes peering directly at me.

Fearful, I slowly stepped back, eyes still fixated on the ones now staring at me. The amplitude of the lights began to grow, and diagonal lines curved inward from the glare, like the deadly eyes of a viper. I knew I didn't have astigmatism. What I was seeing was unreal.

Janice's voice transmitted through the radio again, clearer more than ever this time.

"Joe! Just run! If you can hear me, just run!"

I wasn't paying attention as I kept stepping away, as the incline became too steep from where I stepped off. Before I knew it, I tripped and started to fall backwards, rolling violently down the hill.

Once I'd managed to stop myself, I forced myself up and turned to look behind at the van again. Those eyes… they kept staring into my soul. They were captivating and enticing. But I knew that if I stood there, I probably wouldn't make it…

I ran towards my sister and the other two, as I saw the three of them were now climbing back down and racing my way also. I ran faster than I ever had before. I don't know what was back there or what energy was inside the van, but I refused to look again for another second as I kept running towards the three of them.

When I finally reached them, Janice ran to me and tightly hugged me, squeezing the air from my lungs.

"Thank you, God," she cried. "Oh, thank you."

"What the hell happened?" Kenneth said.

I shook my head frantically. "I-I don't know."

"Did you see something?" Matt asked Janice.

She didn't answer either one of them. She instead kept hugging me tightly, relieved that I was okay. And to think I was more worried about her.

•••

We decided that it was time to go, and hit the road again very shortly after. Janice and I just wanted to get the hell out of there, and undoubtedly, so did Matt and Kenneth after us causing such a commotion. We contemplated whether we should keep on going with the trip and try to make it to the real Bell Rock, but it was still undecided. At this point, we had enough adventure, and likewise, Matt and Kenneth enough spooks for their podcast for sure.

After some time on the road again, we'd both calmed down, and Janice finally let up the nerve to talk.

"You scared me back there," I said.

"I'm sorry," she said.

"Don't be. I think you might've saved my life. I don't know how, but I just feel it."

Janice stirred, nervously rubbed her arm. It was what she always did when she was troubled by something.

"Why'd you scream?" I asked.

127

She grew fearful again. I didn't know if she would even tell, her mouth opening, then closing, then opening again, until finally mustering the courage to speak.

"Back at the butte, when we were climbing and you called to me, I looked through the binoculars and saw something in the van behind you."

Chills waved throughout my body.

"The lights kept alternating and moving in a weird circle in the van," she continued. "Matt said that they weren't supposed to do that. They were all supposed to just stay whatever color they were. And then they turned solid red… and then I saw a figure in the van. Like, a silhouette of someone… or something. It was peeking back at you. Back at me, too, I think."

"Jesus…" I muttered.

"The lights just blinked and then it was fucking gone. Whatever it was, it just disappeared. I know I'm not crazy, Joe. I know what I saw."

I now realized the answer to Matt's question earlier when I told him about my grandmother's premonition about me, and as to whether Janice shared the same power that the others in the family also held. Whatever presence was near me in the van the whole time, she was fully conscious that it was there. I could only hear it, but she could *see* it.

"I believe you," I assured.

DANDELION

I'd never participated in a group study of any kind before. Some students around campus said there may even be some money involved, mainly just mentioned as an incentive to join in the first place, of course. I volunteered specifically for this one due to the subject matter that its research was geared towards, one that I found a bit fascinating.

Dreams... or, so they advertised. More so the study of how the subconscious works in correlation to our deep-rooted memories.

Dr. Ramirez, looking to be in her mid to late-twenties, explained it all just perfectly, and perhaps in the easiest way it could be.

In the room just ahead of the lab, she gave me a quick rundown of how exactly the machine was going to work. On a dry-erase board, she drew one big near-perfect circle, and inside of it drew another smaller circle. She then pointed at the smaller circle with her marker.

"Let's say this is the Earth," she started. I nodded, following along. "And this," she went on, as she motioned around the bigger circle, "is space and beyond. Everything outside of here is full of endless possibilities, right? You've got your other planets, asteroids, comets, satellites, stars, and so on."

I nodded again, a bit amused with her analogy, wherever it was headed.

She continued. "Now, can you imagine where I might be going with this?" she asked with a skittish smile.

I know she didn't expect me to give her an even remotely correct answer.

"You're gonna send me to space?" I dryly remarked.

She laughed. "Not quite, but I like your sense of humor." At least *she* had one, I thought to myself.

Dr. Ramirez went on to further explain as she drew words over the top rim of each circle, labeling them. She started with the smaller circle.

"This is *you*, essentially," she explained while simultaneously writing the word "conscious" over the top rim. She then moved over to the bigger circle. "And this is also you, but the vaster and more mysterious 'you', if that makes sense."

She proceeded to write the word "Subconscious" on top of the larger one. Thankfully she was a visual demonstrator and I was a visual learner. I remembered a decent bit of this when I took AP Psychology back in high school, but then again, I barely passed AP Psych. Had a great teacher, though.

"Have you ever heard the expression 'as above, so below'?" she asked me.

I suggestively tilted my head. "Here or there, maybe once or twice," I answered.

"Well, the reason I ask is because I like to compare that exact same expression to how the subconscious and conscious works," the doctor went on as she pointed at both words with her marker appropriately. "They are both one and the same, however, they like to work in different ways. As you may already know or at least have some sort of grasp on the topic, your subconscious stores most of your long-term data, you know, those memories that can go further back, or even some as recent as yesterday that your brain just decided to lock away in the back. These things don't require your 'conscious awareness' or immediate focus, right?"

From what I noticed about her so far, Dr. Ramirez liked to talk with her hands, but I must say, she made it work for her. It was rather intriguing.

"Whether it's driving a car, riding a bike, or playing the piano," she continued. "Or heck, even learning a new language. At some point, you had to learn these things for the first time, and they required a great deal of conscious effort, yes?" I nodded. "So, thankfully, our brains have been blessed with the ability to 'learn'." She let out a short laugh. "And so, these memories are stored in our subconscious, where it basically becomes second nature to do these sorts of tasks. You with me so far?"

I nodded again to reassure her. My sandpaper-dry personality probably wasn't helping, but she really did have my full attention. I hope she knew that I wouldn't have volunteered otherwise.

"Now," she started again, but this time drew another medium-sized circle just around the "Conscious"-labeled one, "Our understanding of dreams has always been sort of a mystery to science. Many say they're just random jumbles that our brain picks from our subconscious, whereas some say they're a state of mind that acts independently on its own. Well now, we've learned that both of those answers are… well, *sort of* correct."

She then labeled the circle that surrounded "Consciousness" under the name of "Dream State". The entire diagram was starting to look like a big target, with "Consciousness" in the center, "Dream State" being the inner rim, and "Subconscious" as the outer rim.

"Think of our dreams as the Earth's atmosphere," she said. "Any sort of debris that enters the atmosphere at high speed, such as a meteor or fallen satellite, gets broken up into little pieces before it can cause some serious damage to all of us down below, right? I'm assuming you were awake for science class in school?"

"Eh," I joked. She took it with a laugh, but if only she knew I used to have an issue falling asleep in school as a kid.

"So, our dreams protect us from our subconscious, is that what I'm hearing?"

"Ooh, I like the way you think," the doctor remarked. "I'd like to think of it more like, in a less catastrophic example, that our dreams 'filter' what our subconscious throws at us. Now, there's still debate on whether or not our subconscious actively tries to communicate with us or our dreams are the ones pulling from our subconscious, but that's beside the point. What we've come to learn, in the midst of all the chaos in our dream state, from being able to fly, seeing the sky turn a different color, seeing giant chickens cross the road, and whatever other crazy things people have mustered from their imagination is that dreams are no longer the barrier that stands between understanding our subconscious. We've now developed a way to essentially enter our subconscious state, unfiltered and uninterrupted."

And that was where she threw me for a loop. I stammered to try and find the words to even begin questioning something so bizarre, but with no luck. I could tell she was amused by my bafflement from the grin on her face. We'd come so far in technology and scientific advances - was this it? Is this what the future held all this time?

"So, Mr. Thompson," Dr. Ramirez spoke. "Are you ready to explore space?"

• • •

She led me to the lab room where we would be doing our first session of the experiment. The setup was quite complex and intricate for a mere voluntary study for college students. An operating stool sat in the center as expected, and next to it stood a monitor that I assumed was for checking my pulse. Along the wall was the real sight to behold. Large screens displaying all sorts of numbers and diagrams in which I couldn't even comprehend their meaning. Though, from what I could probably guess, it looked like some sort of EEG setup. I'd seen it in movies and documentaries (and back in AP Psych class), but never in person.

"Now before we start, I have to ask if you've eaten in the past 8 hours?" Dr. Ramirez asked. "It's a precaution we take for all of our test subjects due to the side effect of leaving the Hub."

"Uh, just a protein bar," I said. "Did you say 'Hub'?"

"Oh, yes, that's sort of the nickname we came up with for what's basically the 'subconscious state.'"

"Hmm," I nodded.

"So that's good that you've had some form of sugar and carbs at least today. Sometimes people report feeling a bit lightheaded or lethargic after the session, and the first thing they'll usually want is a coffee or a soda. We have a vending machine for soda, snacks, or coffee - whichever you prefer - across the hall if you need them afterwards."

All this time we had discussed going from point A to B, but not *how*. Looking around the room, seeing all the tech being used, I couldn't imagine the funding that must've been poured into this project.

"I'm sure you'll get to it soon enough, but how exactly does this work?" I finally asked, doing my best not to sound impatient. Dr. Ramirez, however, seemed more than happy to explain.

"I thought you'd never ask," she replied. "Well let me just give you a basic rundown of what this all does and how it's going to affect *you*."

She picked up a small lightweight device from the table that clearly looked like some sort of headset, much akin to a VR one. However, it had a sort of synthetic material cap attached to it, with multiple white dot-like pieces carefully placed. It certainly looked like an EEG device for scanning the brain, as I'd guessed earlier.

"This is why we're here today," said Ramirez, pointing at the device with her free hand. "This little guy here is called the Caduceus." I cocked a brow. "Supposedly it's derivative of Hermes' staff, you know, in mythology, the symbol used for ambulances and medical-related stuff?"

"Oh, I see," I acknowledged.

She then handed me the set for me to get a feel for it and analyze it for myself. Nifty, needless to say. As she had explained, the device was capable of not (as she greatly stressed) recording your dreams, per se, but instead recording while simultaneously taking you into your 'subconscious' world. Dreams are merely the barrier blocking us from seeing our subconscious thoughts and memories uninterrupted. In dreams, situations and objects might change sporadically at any given time without warning. One of the greatest struggles, she explained, when testing the Caduceus was trying to find the breakthrough in exactly how to bypass the REM cycle, which is when most of our dreaming occurs. But she explained that as well...

"In the world of science and medicine, or rather human innovation as a whole, we've learned how to basically pick certain parts of our brain and utilize them how *we* see fit, and not the other way around," she preached. "Not have *them* decide for us. Essentially, Caduceus allows us to hack certain parts of the brain that are responsible for letting us take a peek inside our deepest embedded memories. I like to tell people the closest thing we have to a time machine is our own brain. In it lies a whole world of events and moments that you may have forgotten, or choose to have forgotten."

"So what's to stop it from peeking into memories that are… I don't know, better left forgotten?" I proposed. Of course, she had an answer for that as well.

"Great question. So, the beauty of Caduceus is that just like I mentioned, you now have the utmost control over what you decide to see… or, at least we're testing to make sure things stay that way."

And there it was. That was the catch. After all, nothing was ever perfect.

"I'm sorry, I just have to ask, how many people have you tested this thing on?" I boldly inquired.

Ramirez seemed unbothered by the question, though. In fact, nothing seemed to bother her with anything I asked. To me, it conveyed confidence in the things she spoke on, which I hoped also equated to her being sincere.

She chuckled. "Honest answer? About twenty-four so far. Now I'm sure the real reason you're asking is because you want to know how many of those tests turned out successful or not, yeah?"

I answered with a guilty smirk. "Of course not," I joked.

"Well, you have nothing to worry about, Mr. Thompson," she reassured. "All of the people who've participated so far haven't reported any negative side effects, other than the low energy blunder right after the exiting the Hub. So, you're not gonna have to worry about spazzing out or going 'mental' in any sort of fashion. And keep in mind, these tests were done over the course of weeks, and some even months, depending on whether or not we came across more interesting findings during the sessions."

She really didn't back down from a fight. Ramirez stuck to her facts, despite how truthful or not they were, unbeknownst to me.

"You said that everything I'd see in the Hub would be recorded, right?" I mentioned.

"Yes," she confirmed. "They can be transferred over to a small flash drive, if you wish, or we can send directly via email so you can keep it saved on your computer. Only viewable to you. I myself, nor are any other personnel authorized to view your experience – *without* your consent. Only you have the right to grant full permission to us to further help for research purposes. The only real exception to the rule where things start bleeding into the grey area, particularly in stepping past the confines of law, might be whatever warrants probable cause – confession to a crime, for example."

"Huh," I raised my eyebrows. "That'd be unfortunate."

"Are you saying that because you have something you'd like to confess, Mr. Thompson?"

Oh, she had jokes. A good sense of humor indeed.

"I plead the fifth," I retorted. Thankfully, she laughed.

"Well, like I said, if you absolutely want to keep your information and viewings private for your eyes only, that's totally up to you. No pressure, cool?"

I nodded, taking in a short tense breath, then exhaled.

"All right, but you have to promise me one thing," I said.

"Yeah?"

"Call me Travis. If I'm supposed to trust you with handling my brain, we oughta start getting to know each other a little better, don't you agree?"

Respecting my candor, she gave me a pleasing nod. "Fair enough," she replied. "In that case, you may call me Jennifer."

◆◆◆

The Caduceus was now all set, and we were ready to start. The headset over my eyes, electrodes covering my scalp, and the HRM hooked to my wrist and chest were all properly configured. Jennifer also had everything she needed set up on her giant monitor, where she could now see the full scope of my brain, able to pinpoint any changes in activity. From my perspective, the Caduceus headset made everything in the room look like I was peering through a fish-eye lens scope, making my vision blurred and a bit disoriented, but it wouldn't be for long once I entered the Hub, Jennifer informed me.

"You ready?" she asked, sounding more excited than I was.

"Sure," I answered, lying through my teeth.

"Oh yeah? 'Cause from the looks of it, you seem pretty nervous."

I knew she had to be looking at my heartbeat to know that. Considering my inability to hold a poker face, however, perhaps she didn't need to.

"It's okay, everyone experiences the same thing," she added before I could say anything. "Just try to relax. Remember, it's not like a dream where you have no sort of control over what happens to you. You'll have control over the things you experience just like you would in the comfort of your own home, based on the words that I give you. You don't have to see something scary if you don't want to. Remember that, okay?"

I took a deep breath. "Okay," I complied.

"Good." She gave me a pat on the shoulder and walked back over to her desk by her computer and giant monitor. "Alright, so what I'm gonna do is I'm gonna have you count down to 'one', starting from 'five' when I say so. Sound good?"

"Ready when you are," I answered.

"Alright…"

I couldn't see her really from the corner of my goggles, but I could hear her hit a few keys on her computer, along with two clicks of her mouse.

"Okay..." she started.

And with one final click of her mouse, a high-pitched whirring sound began to emit from the Caduceus and straight into both of my ears. It reminded me of the times I had to get a hearing test done, and all those high-frequency noises sounding from left to right.

"Go ahead and countdown for me," she said.

"Five," I began. "Four. Three. Two-"

•••

I'm not sure how quickly it all happened, but the next thing I knew, I was suddenly standing alone in the center of some vast blackness of space, as I opened my eyes. The only light came from above in the form of what I could only describe as a stage spotlight, which shined down on me. I didn't have the sensation that I was dreaming, though. I felt fully present and aware of the fact that I didn't even finish my countdown. Just moments ago, I thought, the last number I was on was 'two.' And now this is where I was. Not laying in the chair of the lab room, no headset or goggles covering my face.

Then a faint, echoey voice sounded from no particular location. It seemed to come from everywhere.

"Travis, can you hear me?" it spoke. *"This is Jennifer. If you can hear me, just go ahead and say something."*

Amazing. She wasn't kidding. It's as if she were God herself speaking to me.

"Yeah..." I answered unsurely. "Can you hear *me*?"

"Perfect, I hear you just fine," Jennifer spoke back from the 'beyond'.

This was a bit too trippy for me. I really didn't know what to expect, but this exceeded anything I could've possibly rehearsed prior in my head.

"You never did count to one," she joked.

"Oh yeah, um... *one*," I remarked. I could even hear her laugh just the same as if she were right next to me. Her voice began to sound more and more clear as she kept talking.

"There we go. Now tell me, right now, what is it that you see?"

Not a damn thing, I wanted to say. But I gave her what I could.

"Well…" I began, looking all around me, still under the spotlight, "I'm standing in… what I *think* is a stage, and there's like…" I looked directly up, "... a spotlight right over me."

"Interesting," I heard Jennifer say. *"That's a new one for me."*

"Where am I?" I asked.

"So, you're actually in 'the Hub' as we speak. This is just your *interpretation of it."*

"My interpretation?"

"Uh-huh. So what happens is that basically, our own subconscious mind presents itself to us through its own unique layout, or environment, if you will. For instance, every time I went through it, I was always standing in a giant ocean of shallow water, and a bright blue sky with no sun in sight. Others

146

see a never-ending field of grass, a barren desert, or maybe even an empty warehouse, in some cases."

"Huh…" I quietly mumbled.

"So for you, your subconscious presents itself in the form of an unlit stage, probably waiting to be filled."

I expected to be more afraid, given that there was basically a never-ending plain of darkness beyond the spotlight, but to my own surprise, I found it a bit peaceful. It also helped that Jennifer was still with me.

"Your vitals appear to be in great shape, which is good. Means your body is responding well to the Caduceus so far. And on that note, I'm gonna begin going down our list of 'sensory triggers'.

I wish she had picked a less threatening word than 'triggers,' especially when I'm in a place so foreign to me (ironic, given that it *is* me).

"How this is going to work is that I'm going to give you a word, and with that word, I want you to close your eyes and concentrate as much as you can on connecting that word to a specific thought or

147

memory, okay? It sounds odd, I know, but trust me, you'll see pretty soon. Don't overthink it."

"Well, I trusted you this far, haven't I?" I remarked.

"Yes, indeed you have, and I'm thankful for that. Okay, so the first word I'm going to give you is… 'golf.'"

"Okay," I spoke under my breath, as I began to close my eyes.

I visualized everything that I possibly could relating to golf, all the way from a golf ball, to Tiger Woods, to a golf club, then to a field of low-cut grass, to a golf cart, and so on. I did this for about five seconds before opening my eyes again. When I opened them, I was met with what I could only describe as the piece of a house set design. It truly was like I was on the stage for a film studio or theater. The set design only showed an open door and small portions of the perimeters of the walls of the structure. It was as if someone cut a portion of the house like a layer of cake, particularly the front door, and placed it in front of me.

"Do you see anything?" Jennifer's voice asked.

I saw something, alright. The problem was, I didn't exactly know what. Obviously, it was a house, but an incomplete one.

"Uh, I see… a part of a house," I said. "Like, it sort of looks like those half-built set houses that you see on film sets, you know, like for shows or movies?"

"Oh, I see. Interesting… Your subconscious mind must be very, hmm… imaginative? Or strongly connected to the cinematic or theatrical."

"Hmmm... it's a theory."

"Hey, no one knows you better than yourself, right?"

I shrugged. "I guess."

"I'm not trying to intrude or anything, this is just me taking notes to see if there's perhaps a correlation between your own personal awareness and how your subconscious views itself, does that make sense?"

"Yep." Sort of, anyway.

"And absolutely if at any point you see something that you'd be more comfortable not sharing with me

and just rather keep to yourself, by all means, you have every right to do so."

"Got it," I concurred.

"Okay, so go ahead and do me a favor and try to describe the house to me. Or what you can of it, at least."

"Well, the door is open," I started.

"What's the door look like?"

I shrugged. "I mean… it's just a regular door. Brown, wooden, has a peephole and everything. Nothing too unordinary."

"Okay… what else?"

From the brief pauses in between her sentences, I could tell she was taking notes.

"Um, from the portion of the house that I *can* see," I continued, "it's made out of wood instead of brick. Light-blue wood, to be exact. I can see a small little porch light perched in the corner, like just before the wall cut off."

There was a brief awkward silence in between, which I assumed was my cue to keep talking while Jennifer kept writing things down.

"And…" I started again, this time trying to peer into the house through the open door. Oddly, I could see that there was an abundant amount of space between the open 'stage' and the inside of the set design house. From where I was standing just several feet away, there appeared to be stairs leading up to a second floor, and a bit to the right was a living room with a couch and perhaps other furniture hidden from view, and beyond, a small hallway leading to what looked to be a kitchen, and maybe even a backyard door and other rooms.

Physically, it didn't actually make sense. There was no way for there to be all that space in between here and there. It was like looking through a portal, essentially, where the space in which I stood didn't proportionally match the one in which I was viewing. I liked to call it the 'small house, big space' phenomenon. But this was something else entirely…

"It looks like I can go inside the house," I finished.

"Well, what are you waiting for?" Jennifer replied. *"Do you want to?"*

I didn't seem to have anywhere else to go, so it seemed to be my only real option.

"Here goes," I shrugged.

I went ahead and walked towards the open door, my view of the inside space growing more and more visible. Once I made it inside, an overwhelming sensation that I couldn't quite put my finger on started to overtake me. It wasn't fear, it wasn't joy, it wasn't sadness… yet, in a strange way, it was almost all three of those things at once.

The house was well-lit in all spaces and corners, quite impossibly, given that there wasn't enough light on the ceilings to emit such radiance. In fact, there didn't seem to be a real source for light at all, as the one on the ceiling wasn't even on. The house just emitted a sort of white luminescence, the kind I'd normally see from plasma beam lights in bathrooms at gas station stops, and I could practically hear that low endless buzzing hum that filled the space. But this time, I didn't hear a noise at all. Silence filled the house instead. Pure silence. That was the only unnerving thing. Even odder, I couldn't even hear my own heartbeat or breathing. Only the sound of my footsteps emerged here and there whenever I made a move across the wooden floor, leaving behind a faint echo, but that was it.

Taking in the overall atmosphere and setup of the house, for some reason, I felt as though I could guess, or even most certainly *knew* the time period in which the interior currently reflected. Perhaps late nineties to early 2000s. I wasn't exactly sure on the year, but I just had a strange certitude of that particular era. Beige walls, carpeted flooring, and brown wooden kitchen cabinets all in a very particular layout that just seemed 'dated.'

"See anything interesting?" Jennifer asked.

"Well, if that's the word you wanna use to describe this," I muttered.

"Just say the first thing that's on your mind."

I looked around, trying to find the first thing I could to catch my eye. But something was extremely off about the house apart from its age. It's as if I knew this place, but yet I couldn't understand how. The smell even brought about a strange sense of familiarity. A faint scent of-

"Lavender," I said. "It smells like lavender."

There was a brief pause. Then Jennifer finally spoke. *"Tell me, does the lavender scent mean anything to*

you? Maybe, bring you back to a certain time or place?"

"I... I think so. I'm not sure how, though."

"What else can you tell me about the house?"

I peeked around again.

"There's a corded phone sitting on a stand, next to a lamp and a recliner," I said.

"Corded, huh?"

"Yeah, corded."

"Does the house seem a bit... outdated? Or from a different time than present-day?"

Now it was as if she could read my mind.

"Yeah, that's about right," I said. "You know how some houses just look old? Like houses they just don't make anymore?"
I heard Jennifer let out a small chortle. *"I know exactly what you mean."*

I shook my head confusingly. "But it's like I know this place somehow," I added.

"Well Travis, even though you nor myself know exactly where it is you are, I can tell you this. What you're standing in right now is likely an old memory you've forgotten, stored into the far reaches of your subconscious. You have *been to this place before. This is your subconscious's best replication and rendering - if you will - of the memory in a way that makes sense to you."* And yet, it didn't make sense at the same time. *"Can you see any pictures posted along the walls or perhaps over a fireplace anywhere?"*

There actually was a fireplace in the living room, and plenty of picture frames. But there were no pictures. Not a single one in any of the big, small, and portrait-sized frames set throughout the house. Yet, they were all carefully positioned as though there were supposed to be photos within the frames for people to see.

"As a matter of fact, I don't," I answered, puzzled.

"I see," Jennifer responded. *"So as odd as that may seem, it's actually a common thing people who've used the Caduceus report about seeing in 'the Hub', or I guess I should say 'not see', in this case. Faces and actual people are a bit more difficult to render and replicate from stored memory banks. Over time,*

you forget exactly how someone's face actually looks. You have an idea of how they appear, but you can't actually remember all the fine details, such as exact facial structure, moles, size between the eyes, you name it. That's why dreams tend to do a better job at showing you people you've seen more recently in your everyday life. But you realize that even in your dreams where you might see pictures of actual people, or people you've never even met before, notice how you can't seem to remember exactly what they look like once you wake up? Only a broad description, like skin color, eye color, hair, height, sex, and so on?"

I knew the feeling all too well. It was a bit uncanny, if I'm being honest. The least my imagination could do was make up some pictures, I would think, at least just to fill the void. This was just flat out strange…

"Why can't my subconscious just make something up, like how my dreams do?" I asked.

"Great question. This is where I have to break it to most people. Your imagination is practically meaningless in the Hub. Scientists, psychologists and other scholars from all over within the profession have started to come to the understanding that dreams and the imagination have

*more in common with each other than our
subconscious and the imagination. The subconscious
is more concrete and based on what actually
happened, whereas dreams and the imagination
focus on what could be, and possibly what can
happen. So, if the subconscious can't actually
remember something, it won't be able to render it in
the Hub. That's often why most subjects just see
places and certain structures rather than actual
people. Those things are easier for the mind to pick
up on and remember to the best of detail."*

"And, if it's a dream that I remember?" I questioned.

"I'm sorry?"

"What if what I'm remembering is a dream? Like,
that still actually happened, right? Not literally in the
real world, but it's still real to me, you know?"

*"Well, Travis, that's what we're here for. Yes,
absolutely a dream is still a real memory. That's
why we still think about them and can describe them
to others after we've woken up. That being said, the
whole chaotic disorientation of dreams occurs due
to what again?"*

Again, I understood, as I nodded, answering, "Our
subconscious."

"Bingo. Our subconscious is constantly trying to tell us something, whether we choose to ignore it or not. The Caduceus breaks down exactly what that is."

The longer I stood in this place, the more it gradually began feeling as though I were standing in a vacuum of space, with no real sense of time or reality. Where was I? How did this all come to be just from the word 'golf'?

"Try exploring the house a bit more," Jennifer suggested. *"See if that does anything."*

I headed upstairs. Plastered along the walls leading up the stairs and beyond was a fully encompassing floral-design wallpaper. It was a very particular floral design, enough to bring back that sensation I felt earlier when I first stepped in the house...

"I've seen this wallpaper before," I whispered, as I dragged my palm across the walls going up the stairs.

When I got to the top, I saw that the upstairs room was set up to be used for a game room. Oddly, the contrast in this room stood out from the downstairs. Small and ever-so-dim corners and shadows placed about the room reminded me of old photos that people used to take on those polaroid cameras from the 80s and 90s. It had a grainy look to it, as well as an uneven exposure. This time, though, it seemed as if I were in one of those pictures.

The space was almost entirely bare, except for a small entertainment system which stood against the wall (this one not being covered in floral design), accompanied by a bulky 30 to 35-inch CRT TV, and a Nintendo 64, with a game cartridge sticking up from inside that I couldn't distinguish from this far. My mouth dropped open, astonished, and that excited feeling of electricity, the kind you get when you experience an 'ah-ha' moment, now replaced any other notion of uncertainty that I may have had before.

"Oh my god," I spoke under my breath.

"Travis?" Jennifer's voice spoke.

I let out a short, scoff-like chuckle as I clasped my hands over my head.

"This is my aunt's old house," I exclaimed. "My Aunt Deborah - this is her old house."

"Now we're getting somewhere," Jennifer spoke in a proud tone.

I let out another laugh. "This is insane," I commented. "I remember we visited here one time. A *long* time ago. And…"

I stepped towards the entertainment center, and bent over to get a closer peak at the N64. I now clearly saw what cartridge was inserted into the console, and a smile drew over my face.

"Good ol' country club golf," I finished. "Wow…"

"Country club golf?" Jennifer asked.

"One of the games we used to play on the '64 was *Waialae Country Club.* '*True Golf Classics*', to be exact."

"Ah…"

I could practically hear her taking down notes.

"That's insane…" I whispered under my breath.

"I told you you'd see where I was going with this, huh?" Jennifer teased. *"I hope I've completely sold you on it now."*

"Yeah," I laughed. "Yes you have."

This was something beyond any other thing I've done before. This was bigger than virtual or augmented reality. This was something else entirely. It knew my deepest memories and had made a place inside my own brain. A *real* place.

Jennifer continued. *"You see, these words that I'm giving you is just a small example of what your subconscious can act with, based on just a single word that can trace back to countless other thoughts stored in your memory bank. One word can trigger a labyrinth of random places and memories. We now are starting to understand why we dream something related to a conversation we might've had earlier that same day, and why our brains decided to cling onto that specific conversation or even a single word that was said. Caduceus allows us to do that exact same thing but on our own terms."*

Jennifer allowed me to explore the house a bit more. I tried checking out the other rooms, but each time I was met with nearly empty spaces. I'm not sure how my subconscious mind was trying to interpret the house, but it was the equivalent to a bad buffer, or loading bar that never quite finished. Some rooms had little furniture, and for the furniture that *did* exist, they were weirdly vague.

In different parts of the rooms, it was like a Picasso drawing come to life, just a bit neater and more organized. At least I could tell it was furniture and decor for different sections of the house, yet, I couldn't exactly discern just *what* it was I was looking at. Some things looked like a chair, others like a lamp, maybe even some jewelry lying about, and other sorts of bathroom accessories like a towel or soap made sense here and there, but overall, when you looked at them altogether, the house was an enigma.

"Jennifer, why is everything so…" I began, trying to find the word.

"Disorganized? Jumbled? Confusing?" she finished for me.

"Right."

"So, remember what I told you, just like with the pictures, the Hub can only render and replicate what it knows, or the best idea of what it 'thinks' it knows. What is it in your dream - I'm sorry, subconscious state - *that looks disorienting to you, if I may ask, of course?"*

I let out a short burst laugh. "I wouldn't exactly know how to tell you, you know? Or where to start."

"Do things sort of look like, for example, like they're pieces of furniture or specific objects, yet, they somehow don't at the same time?"

"Yeah, that's exactly what it's like. I don't understand it, though."

"Well, that's what these studies are for, right? What you're doing right now is a huge help to getting us to better understand how our subconscious minds continue to work in mysterious ways. It seems a common testimony in all the people who've participated report the same thing of not being able to completely interpret specific objects. It's a known fact that over time, our brains will remember things much differently than how they actually occurred, and certain memories will slowly fade over the years."

"So, I can still remember the basic layout of the house, but not what was in it specifically?" I guessed.

"Mm-hmm. You got it. So… would you like to continue on to a different word?" Excited now, I agreed. *"Very well then. Just like before, when I say the word, you're gonna close your eyes and just*

focus on every single thing you can related to that word alone. Ready?"

"Ready."

"Okay... 'summer'."

•••

I opened my eyes and was no longer inside. I was outdoors, the sky was clear blue, and it was bright and warm out. Facing my feet, I saw that I was standing on grass, and when I looked back up to see around me, in the distance there were fields of trees that led to deep woods. Not too far to my left lied a small timber bridge just over a tiny creek with a bed full of rocks. It had to be in some sort of park. A summer camp, maybe? Or just perhaps a regular community park I may have visited some time ago.

I walked around to try and see what other things might pop up to spark something inside. As I turned a corner around a field of tall bushes, the scene beyond abruptly changed to that of what looked to be the grounds of a fare or some sort of carnival. A carousel, stuffed prizes, empty concessions, and other sorts of festivities lined up. I remembered a place like this once, I thought.

I told Jennifer all of this, and we both began trying to dig for clues as to what this particular memory was about. However, this one was a lot easier than my Aunt Deborah's house, since I actually can recall this day. Or, at least the fact that we showed up. The only other moments I can maybe remember having on this day were playing tag with some friends, strangers, or even cousins, and us throwing this small toy shovel at a couple of wasp nests just under the timber bridge I'd seen earlier, then running like hell later to escape their fury. Funny how that thought decided to resurface the longer I stayed here. I couldn't imagine doing something so cruel nowadays.

"Hmm, looks like your mood changed a bit," Jennifer pointed out, more than likely reading my vitals again from where she was. *"You seem relaxed. And the parts of your brain that are lighting up more would have me guess that you're experiencing a great sense of joy and happiness. Sound about right?"*

"I miss my childhood," I replied. "Sometimes it'd be great to just relive a time where I didn't have to be an adult, you know?"

"Oh, I hear you. Why don't you say it louder for the people in the back. Nostalgia is what you're feeling

right now, and it's a shared part of the human experience to feel it every once in a while."

I chuckled. But then I stopped as a thought occurred to me.

"Is it normal to not see anybody at all?" I questioned. "In the Hub, I mean?"

"Yes, it's very normal. In very few cases, we've had some people report seeing long-lost family members or even some friends of theirs. When we talked about it after, all of them said that the people they saw in the Hub had a strong relationship with them, which tells us that the stronger the bond we share with people in our lives, the longer we hold onto those memories, allowing us to paint a better picture of how they looked through the Caduceus."

"I guess I don't love anyone as much as I thought," I dryly remarked.

"I'm sure that's not true," Jennifer said, knowing good and well that I was joking. *"It's gonna be different for everyone else. The words that another host or myself gives to you or others won't come up with the same results, obviously because you all have different life experiences and memories unique to yourself."*

It was time to move on to a different 'trigger word', as Jennifer called them. Still wish she would've picked a different name for it, but I digress.

"Alright, you ready?" she started as usual.

"Ready when you are," I replied.

"Good. Okay... 'dandelion'."

•••

As before, I closed, then opened my eyes. I found myself standing in a vast lobby of some sort. There was some light, but very little to illuminate the entire space. The floor was a velvet red-colored carpet. As I looked around at the barely visible walls, an artificial tree standing in a pot in the corner, and another obscure, jumbled rendering of an object that looked gold, I was beginning to think I was standing in a theater lobby of sorts.

I walked ahead to explore, and found myself feeling, for the first time since I initially started, rather uneasy. But I didn't know why...

The area was spacious, and from my perspective, the theater felt as if it could fit hundreds of people. I couldn't tell if I had shrunk some or if the design of the place was just *that* large, but everything felt so gigantic. Unnecessarily gigantic, I should add.

As I kept walking, in the distance I saw a faint shimmer of light grow more and more visible. With each step, I began to realize that it was an over light, or a sort of spotlight, rather. Underneath the light was a random dinner table, perfectly arranged and set up for guests. But why here? It was so strange and out of place. Yet, I began to notice something else even stranger that I didn't acknowledge until now. I didn't hear Jennifer's voice this time.

"Jennifer?" I called out.

No response. There was no hiding it now. I was nervous. Not just nervous that the Caduceus might have malfunctioned, but downright afraid because I was completely alone...

"Jennifer?" I called again.

Still nothing. That uncomfortable silence that filled the Hub was louder than anything. I could hear my own heartbeat frantically pounding between my ears.

"Yes?" Jennifer's voice called back to me. *"Travis, can you hear me?"*

Hearing her voice again was like being thrown in an icy pool of water just to be pulled back out and doused in warm water. Whether it was a simple mishap in the machine or not, it was fucked up regardless.

"You had me worried there for a sec, Jennifer," I spoke as I let out a breathy chuckle of relief.

"Yeah, that was kinda strange. Nothing seemed to show interference on my end... I'm not sure what happened. I was calling to you but I couldn't hear anything back."

And let's add that to the list of 'mistakes' this test run was supposed to catch while we're at it.

"Do you see anything interesting - well, I guess I should ask what do you see?"

I told her about the theater, at least it was what I thought to be a theater, as well as the obscurity of the dinner table. She of course tried to tie this back with the 'theatrical' theme I had going on in my subconscious mind, which I still thought might be a bit of a stretch. For now, she insisted that I kept exploring to see what else I could find that may explain things.

Near the end of the hallway, a door remained ajar, and a shade of light projected from the room in a wedge shape. I'd have to keep walking further to see what was inside, but I couldn't help but feel slightly more uneased. Something didn't feel right about all of this. None of the other settings gave me this sensation.

I carefully stepped into the room with the open door, and was intrigued by what I saw. The scene had changed yet again, this time to what looked to be a party room of some sort. Long tables were aligned with chairs pushed in and spaced apart from each other. Plastic colored cups, paper plates, napkins, and cone-shaped party hats were neatly stacked and perfectly organized along each row. The floor also had a retro-patterned carpet design like the ones I'd see in other theaters or arcades, multi-colored spots and irregular shapes over a black backdrop, making me feel like I was going to space. The lighting in here was different as well. It was a dimly-lit blue ambiance, almost like a night light. I found it rather calming compared to the outside in the theater lobby, though, undeniably odd.

Then from behind me, the deafening sound of the door slamming shut echoed throughout room. I jumped with an overwhelming sensation of dread.

"Travis, are you okay?" Jennifer's voice sounded. *"Your heartbeat's escalating really fast. Is everything all right?"*

I almost forgot how to breathe.

"I-I don't know what just happened," I stammered. "The door shut."

"The door? What door?"

"The one to the party room. I'm inside the party room and the door just slammed. Am I alone? I-Is someone here with me?" I was panicking.

"Travis, remember what we discussed. You don't have to see anything scary if you don't want to. You hear me? You don't have to be afraid. Just take a deep breath, close your eyes, and count to three, okay?"

That was the last thing I wanted to do. I wanted to yell at her to get me out of this damn place. Pick any other goddamn word for all I care. I just wanted to get the hell out of here. There was also the inkling that I maybe wasn't alone after all in the Hub. I hadn't seen a single figure yet, and the first signs of anyone else being here with me began to seem more alarming than I once thought.

I closed my eyes and did what she said.

I sounded off, "1… 2… 3."

I opened my eyes again, and this time, I was still in the party room, but the calming blue luminescence was now replaced with an unsettling crimson instead. The place had turned into a red room. I didn't tell Jennifer, but I hated the color red. It was a lot of people's favorite color, but I never liked it. It made me feel sick, and here I was drowned by its presence.

I looked around and noticed other horrifying features of the room. Streaks of what I could only assume was blood were randomly plastered across different parts. What kind of godawful memory was this?

Anxiety returned. I found it hard to breathe yet again. I needed to get out of here.

"Jennifer, get me out!" I yelled. "You hear me? Jennifer, please get me out!"

This time, she didn't respond. Fuck. It was malfunctioning again. Such bad timing.

"Shit," I muttered. "Shit, shit, shit…"

Panicked, I stood huddled in a corner of the room, not sure of where to go, but definitely not wanting to leave myself exposed to whatever may be out there. I wasn't sure how long I was going to be stuck here, maybe forever for all I knew. But right now wasn't the time to think of any of that. Whatever positive affirmations Jennifer tried to preach clearly wasn't working. I had to be brave, I told myself. It was just my own subconscious. I tried to tell myself that to give me some sort of comfort.

I crept over to the door with nothing to defend myself with. Jennifer wasn't here to accompany me now. I was alone.

When I got to the door, I hesitated to place my hand on the knob. But I slowly raised and positioned it over, and was just about to grasp the knob until I realized something. There was now a window framed onto this door, unlike the first time…

I looked up, and right before my eyes, a child, a small boy, slammed his hands onto the window from the other side, screaming at the top of his lungs. Up until this point, I never experienced something as bone-chilling and hair-raising as the sight before me.

I jumped back, so frightened that I fell to the floor. I kept my eyes fixed on the child, as he continued beating on the window, screaming for help. He was the first person I'd seen in the Hub, and he was so real. So vivid. The fear in his eyes, the franticness... I wanted to help him.
But before I could do anything, something, or someone snatched him away and disappeared from the other side of the door.

"No!" I gasped.

•••

Before I knew it, I was back in the lab room with Jennifer right next to me, frantically removing the Caduceus from off of me. The sterile whiteness of the room blinded me as she removed the headset from my eyes.

I sat in the hallway with Jennifer, discussing what might've gone wrong and why. She wasn't kidding about the side effects that were to occur after. I felt tremors travel throughout my hands and mostly legs.

She gave me a cup of coffee with plenty of creamer and sugar to help me recuperate.

"That should not have happened," she apologized, as she had many times already at this point. "That *definitely* should not have happened."

"It's all right," I insisted.

"No, it's not. I-I don't even know how this happened. It hasn't before."

I rubbed my forehead, still discombobulated with both being in the Hub and from what I just witnessed. Flashes of images depicting the red... the blood... and the god-awful screams.

"I know I told you before that you're not liable or entitled to share anything you've seen during the session with me at all, and that it's entirely confidential, but if you absolutely maybe want to speak with someone-"

"It's fine," I said.

There was a brief awkward pause between us.

"Just take as much time as you need and let me know if you need anything else while you're here, okay?" Jennifer warmly noted. "I don't want to send you home in a distraught state, you know?"

I couldn't tell her. That would make me look suspicious, albeit to a 'crime' or witness to a crime I had no recollection of, to begin with.

"I saw a kid," I continued. "I actually saw someone. It was a boy. And… I tried to save him, but…"

I shut up before I said anything else that might be incriminating. I couldn't believe how visibly upset I was getting. I was angry at the fact that I couldn't do anything to save him, yet horrified by whatever thing I saw that took him away. Who or what, I don't know.

"Was it anyone you recognized?" Jennifer asked.

I shook my head. "No. No…"

"Travis, I'm not legally allowed to exploit or share any other information outside of the experiment," Jennifer said. "For the sake of your confidentiality. It was part of the agreement you signed before we began, and for good reason. Same with the footage that was recorded. I recommend keeping it for yourself in the meantime just to be safe. Trust me, if there was anything else I could do to help you understand this better, I would. Believe me, I would."

I nodded. But in truth, I didn't know anything. I didn't know anything about that memory at all. I don't even know where I was, who I saw, or what party I was there for. In fact, I don't remember going to anyone's party at all as a kid. What did I see? Was it even a real memory?

•••

A week had passed since the incident, and I still had nothing to go off of. Only the flash drive containing the session that Jennifer had given me to hold on to for safe keeping. A big part of that was mostly due to me not wanting to broadcast it to anyone, not even my own family. Gradually, I began to start forgetting about the ordeal almost entirely.

Almost.

I paid my mother a visit over the weekend. She was still single after all these years. It made me wonder how much in love she must've been with my dad, or how much the opposite, given that she didn't bother to try and date or see other people. Props to her, though, she did just fine on her own. I was her only child, so after I left the house, it was all peace and quiet from there. She was fixing me some of her famous buffalo chicken casserole. It was her hit special she always made for potlucks and other get-togethers. The neighbors loved it and so did all my friends when we were growing up.

"You seem… off," she mentioned, cocking a brow. "Everything okay?"

I couldn't lie to her. One, I'm not great at it, as I didn't care to, and two, my mother was good at knowing when I did.

"Did I mention to you at all in the past couple of weeks about me signing up to be a part of this, uh… experiment, group study type-of-thing?" I said, easing into it.

She shook her head. "I don't think so. What kind of experiment?"

"Well, that's where it gets interesting."

She gave an odd, dumbfounded look as she walked over to the table, placing a fork and plate full of hot casserole down in front of me along with a glass of Kool-Aid. The smell of the casserole alone was enough to ease my mind, just a bit.

"You still have… everything intact the way it was when I pushed you out of me, right?" she joked with a dry expression.

She had jokes, even with her bland sense of humor.

"Yes, Mother, nothing like that," I reassured her, rolling my eyes.

"Okay," she said, putting her hands up. She took a seat in the chair adjacent to me, where we could both see each other in full. She wore her usual gown and slippers and had her hair tied back. She looked about as 'motherly' as a mother could look.

I took a bite from my food, relishing in its taste for as long as I could before spilling the details.

"This test…" I started, talking between chewing food in my mouth, "It uses a machine to look into your 'subconscious', basically. It sees all your long-forgotten or even suppressed memories, as if you're really there in vivid detail, kinda like a dream. Of course, they aren't allowed to see anything for my privacy's sake, but I can see everything."

I'd expected her to maybe share some ounce of curiosity or enthusiasm. Her face, however, remained distractingly deadpan to the point of unease.

"Oh," she uttered.

"It's completely safe," I remarked, feeling as if that were a lie. "They tested it on a bunch of other people before and so far nothing bad happened to them."

My mother was still silent.

"It was pretty cool," I continued. "I mean, for the first bit, anyways."

She finally spoke. "Well, what did you see?"

I hesitated, taking a sip of my drink. "Different things. Aunt Deborah's old house, you know, her blue one she used to have?"

Again, I was expecting a more amazed reaction from her, but my mother kept her same dull skepticism.

"That was so long ago," she said. "How could you remember that?"

I smirked. "That's the thing, mom. This device, the Caduceus, is what they call it, it can see everything. It brings back all sorts of memories in near-perfect detail just from the trigger of a single word they give you. The word 'balloon' might trigger a bunch of things right here in your brain," I said, pointing at my temple, "and bring you back to a specific moment in time relating to that word, no matter how unrelated it may be. It's crazy, right?"

Yet, I still sounded more excited than what she showed. "What did you mean it was good for the first half?" she spoke, almost ignoring everything I just said.

Then my level of enthusiasm matched hers. Practically nonexistent.

"Well, just the same way I saw some cool things, like, stuff I couldn't have remembered from forever ago," I said, "... There were also some not so fun things I saw."

The still concern in my mom's face now started to escalate into anxiety. Her eyes told all.

"It was… like a nightmare," I went on. "I felt trapped for a bit. But thankfully they managed to pull me out."

"Well, what did you see that was scary?" she asked.

Again, I hesitated. For what? She was my mother. I hadn't shared it with anyone else, but this would be the time to finally tell-all, I thought to myself.

"I saw this boy," I started. "And he looked scared. And… it scared *me*. I don't know what happened after that, but soon they got me out of the simulation."

"Oh…" she lowly uttered. "Was it anyone you'd seen before?"

That was a good question. "I don't know," I answered honestly. "But I don't wanna do that again. They tried to call me the other day, asking if I wanted to continue with the testing to look more into it, but honestly, screw that."

My mother then stood up to walk back into the kitchen. "Well good," she said. "I don't think it's a good idea either to keep going to those people. Especially something in early development like that. You never know what might go wrong. You don't know if that thing might, I don't know, give you an aneurysm or something."

She wasn't wrong. Then again, she's always been a bit 'overprotective' of me, more than any other parent I'd met.

•••

In our attic, I was helping her take down old Christmas decorations, putting the lights and ornaments in the proper boxes we'd kept for years. I took it upon myself to give my mom a hand, which she said I didn't have to do, but I insisted. Sorting through it all was kind of hectic, given that there was a lot of shit we just kept up there for absolutely no reason. If no one could tell my mother was a hoarder, all they'd have to do was look in her attic and they'd know. Between sorting through all the decorations, I took small breaks.

During that time, I would look through other things in the countless boxes my mom kept, peeping at old memories and things of hers even before my time. Her old prom photo, pictures of her childhood, my grandparents when they were younger. And there was me. Pictures of me when I was a baby and in kindergarten showed up. Old activities like my painted handprint, macaroni art, colorings, and other sorts of things were there. Eventually, I became engrossed in delving into the past.

I continued flipping through the stacks of photos, and then I came across one that stuck out to me. It was of my mom and another man, and in the background was Aunt Deborah's house, just like it had appeared in the Hub. The blue exterior and the porchlight both looked the exact same. But who was the man Mom was with? They looked like they were together, given that they both were holding each other a bit close.

My first guess was my dad, a man I never met. I mean, he kinda looked like me. It would make the most sense for it to be him. But then I looked at the date stamp at the bottom of the picture. The picture was taken on *June 6th, 2000.*

I was confused. I would've been six-years-old already. My birthday is April 23rd, '94. Yet, my dad was in this picture and well with my mom, and I was already about to pass kindergarten into first grade if I did the math correctly. How could I not remember my own father?

I captured a photo of this one with my phone to have a copy for myself. I put it back exactly the way I found it so my mother wouldn't suspect anything. But still, why should she even lie about something like that? She said they divorced before I was even old enough to remember. Clearly, that wasn't at all true.

Now I was curious. I kept going through all the other pictures I could find, mostly of me or my mom, seeing if there were any other date stamps on them at the bottom. I didn't have too much luck at first. Most of them were just random pictures of me from my childhood. Me riding my bike, playing at the park, climbing trees, you know, those sorts of things. Some of them didn't even have dates on them, but given the vague context of the photos, it didn't matter regardless, as they gave me little to work with.

Come to think of it, I have no recollection of my mom, or whoever, even taking these pictures when they happened. I get that it was so long ago, but the moment they were captured, I figured I'd have at least some remembrance of what I was doing and where I was.

And just when I came to the ones at the bottom once again, I struck gold. This one didn't have a date stamp, but the picture spoke a thousand words. It was me at a birthday party. *My* birthday party. I knew because I was the one blowing out the candles in the picture. Looking at the cake and the candle stuck into it, I saw that I just turned seven. And then I noticed the background. Chills coursed all throughout my body.

The party room from the Caduceus. It was the exact same. Down to nearly every detail. The cups, plates, the arrangement of the tables, the walls, carpeted floor pattern, the spacing...

I took another photo with my phone, but just before I was about to put it down, I saw something else that left me frozen. Just to the left of me was a young boy who looked all too familiar. Of course, I thought. That was him. That was the boy I saw in the Caduceus. That was the boy I saw screaming for his life.

•••

I came back down from the attic and met my mother in the living room, who was watching TV. I decided to show her the photo of me at the birthday party. I figured showing the one of her and what I suspected to be my father would be a lot more contentious, so best not to even bring it up. I held the polaroid out to where the image would face her.

"Where did you find this?" she asked, as she took the photo from me.

Where do you think? I thought to myself. "I found it in the attic," I said. "Along with the other stuff. I was just looking through old pictures. Pictures of us, and you." My mom stayed fixated on the picture. "You looked really pretty in your prom dress, Ma."

But she didn't say anything. Just kept on looking at the photo, as if it were peering right back at her. The longer the moment dragged the more awkward I began to feel.

"Yeah," she finally said in a low whisper. "Yeah, that was your, uh… seventh birthday."

Thoughts of what might've happened that day began to race through my mind based on my mother's tone. She knew something. Did she and my dad get into a fight? Was there a dispute with one of the other parents? And then I totally forgot to ask-

"Do you know who that kid is in the picture next to me?" I questioned. "The one on the left."

She glanced at me, then back at the photo, staring at it again in that same bizarre manner.

"I… don't remember," she answered. "I'm pretty sure he was a friend of one of the other kids in the neighborhood, or maybe from your class. There were a lot of parents there that day and some of my friends invited their kids over, so maybe he was one of them?"

Then why would he be sitting directly next to me? Maybe I was looking too much into it, but I would've figured that either siblings, cousins, or even a best friend would want to sit next to the birthday boy while he blew out his candles. Or maybe, he really was a stranger. Whoever he was, he clearly left a hell of an impression on me to stay imprinted in my memories for so long.

Needless to say, I didn't believe her. She also never gave that photo back to me, but that was fine. I had my own digital copy now.

•••

Later I'd fallen asleep at her place in my old room. I had a terrible nightmare. I was back in the party room. It was red again. Red everywhere. The blood streaks on the wall were all there as well. It was like a repeat of what I already saw, a recurring dream, in this case. Compared to the Caduceus experience, this felt more like an actual REM cycle dream, whereas in the Caduceus I was almost *too* aware of what was going on. I hadn't dreamed about the experience at all since the last time, and I wondered how that was so. Usually, something that was on my mind or worried me in secret tended to show itself through my dreams.

I got out of my bed and walked out into the hall leading to the living room. The TV was still on, as the faint light and sound traveled up the walls as I made my way closer. I peeked my head to see if my mom was still on the couch. She'd fallen asleep right where she was with the TV on in the background.

I decided to go back up to the attic and search for more photos that may give a clue. Once I made it to the top, I turned on the light and looked towards the direction of the boxes I stumbled across earlier.

They were now gone.

•••

The next day I'd given Jennifer a call. I called her desk number, to which thankfully, she answered.

"Dr. Ramirez speaking," she spoke.

"Hi, Dr. Ramirez. It's Travis," I answered back.

"Travis," she said, sounding pleased to hear my voice. "How've you been?"

"Better, much better, all things considered," I remarked.

"Well good. I'm glad to hear that."

"I was actually calling to see about… using the Caduceus again."

•••

The next week it was back to where it started. I met with Jennifer again and she had the whole procedure set up like last time. I once again sat in the chair and the Caduceus hooked to my scalp and over my eyes.

"Okay, we're gonna start things a little slow like last time in order for me to follow a pattern," Jennifer informed me. "If we can maybe pinpoint when and where something went wrong with a similar list of triggers I gave you, that might give us some answers. Sound good to you?"

I shrugged. "I guess."

"I know that's not comforting, but trust me, you're helping us more than you know by coming back here."

She had a point. I *did* come back here. No one forced me to. "Also, I think I found a better word for what you and the other participants might have been experiencing," she added. "Liminal spaces." I arched an eyebrow. "Think of them as voids or shells of open spaces, complexes, structures, rooms, and so on, that usually are full of people or life, but instead have no remnants of them whatsoever. That's why it may feel strange to be so alone in the Hub, wouldn't you agree?"

I nodded. "That would explain the studio look," I remarked.

"Exactly. Alright, you ready?" she asked.

"Uh-huh," I answered.

"Any questions or concerns before we begin?"

I shook my head. "Beam me up, Scotty," I dryly humored.

Like before, she counted from five, then before she could even get to one, I was already transported into 'the Hub.' Nothing really changed. It was the usual black void with a faint stage light directly over me, or like standing under a streetlight on a dark sidewalk. This time, she began with a different word.

Bicycle.

•••

I did as instructed and closed my eyes. When I opened them, I was now standing on a sidewalk for real this time, except it was daytime, and I was in a neighborhood. Green grass, brown fences; it was your typical suburban district... and one that I inexplicably recognized.

"What do you see, Travis?" Jennifer asked.

And I told her just that. But I knew this place. Somehow, though, unbeknownst to me, it felt familiar, more so than Aunt Deborah's house that took longer for me to process.

"I'm in a nice neighborhood," I spoke.

"Look familiar at all? Anything distinct that catches your eye?"

"No, but it looks like I've been here before. Well, I *know* I've been here before, of course, but I feel like I recognize this place."

I began to take a step down the sidewalk, but stopped when I realized where I remembered the scene from. When I went through the old photos from my mom's attic and came across the ones of me when I was a kid, I recall one that had no date stamped at the bottom, but the scenery in the background was that of this particular neighborhood, no doubt, and I was riding my bicycle. But that memory was fairly recent, was it not?

"Well damn," I whispered.

"Travis?" Jennifer's voice called to me.

"I came across some old pictures the other week, and lo and behold, this place was in one of them. When you said 'bicycle', that explained a lot."

"What do you see?"

"A neighborhood. A regular suburban neighborhood. It's sunny outside. Empty, of course. But pleasant."

"Were you riding a bicycle in the picture?"

"Sure was. My mom took the photo-

But did she? my conscience spoke to me.

"And I know I had to be around four or five-

Did you know that for sure?

"Maybe… but I saw the picture not too long ago, like last week. Why is it showing up here now?"

"Well, do you think it wouldn't have shown up had you not come across the photo recently?" Jennifer proposed.

It was hard to say.

"You see," she continued, "the subconscious is weird like that, where you might dream about something that occurred earlier in the day, or sometimes a random memory that could be from days, weeks, or even years before. Or even, something that's on your mind."

And something *was* on my mind.

"Jennifer, can I ask a favor?" I said.

"Sure."

"Can I recommend a certain trigger word?"

There was a brief pause. Though I couldn't see her face from here, I could just sense she wasn't open to the idea. She was the doctor, after all.

"What did you have in mind?" she responded, to my surprise.

I didn't know what to say, given that I didn't think my suggestion would even work. I really just wanted to know about the boy in the photo. If I was here in the neighborhood now, maybe I could use that to my advantage.

"I was thinking about maybe going back to the party room?"

The idea frightened me by just even asking. It was the last place I wanted to go, but maybe this time I could have more control given that I'd already experienced it and know what to expect. Jennifer said I didn't have to see anything scary if I didn't want to. Maybe things just went awry last time because I suppressed it for so long and I didn't know how to cope with it (whatever 'it' was).

Of course, I was just making assumptions on my own.

"Travis, I don't think that's such a good idea," she seriously advised. *"You know what happened last time. Looking at how your body responded to that moment, I just don't want anything bad to happen to you. You were hyperventilating last time, who's to say you won't have a full-on panic attack or lose control of your breathing altogether this time?"*

The logical part of my brain said she was right. But then again, if only she knew what it was I was trying to accomplish.

"You said I didn't have to see anything scary I didn't want to in the Caduceus, right?" I retorted.

"Right, but-

"Maybe I can control it better this time. I can know what to expect, right?"

"Travis, might I ask, is there a particular reason why you want to go back to that moment?"

Shit, I thought to myself. She was prying.

"Well… let's just say, with what happened last time, and with what I saw... I need some answers." There was silence for a while. "Think you can help me?"

Another brief pause between us.

"Technically I don't have to guide you with these trigger words for your subconscious mind to show you something," Jennifer explained. *"That part of the activity last time was cut short due to obvious reasons, but technically, yes, you can have control over your own experience in the Hub."*

An orb of excitement swelled inside my chest.

"However," Jennifer's voice abruptly sounded again. *"If you're not careful, it can be very dangerous for the subject. Should anything bad happen again this time, I will immediately pull you out. Do I have your consent on that?"*

"Deal," I complied. "So how does this work?"

"You basically will go about it the same way we have been. Instead of me giving you a word, you just close your eyes and focus hard on one particular thought or word yourself, then open them back up and there you have it. The words were just baby steps to see how your brain reacted to it."

"I guess I was the exception."

"Well, that's what we're here to find out. Also, understand that the same words we used before may not render the same results. The word we used last time, umm... bubble gum, I think?"

"Dandelion," I corrected.

"Right, dandelion. That may not bring you to the same memory as before. Your subconscious might search for a multitude of memories based off of that one word, or whatever seems more pressing at the time."

"Last time you weren't able to hear me and I wasn't able to hear you. What if that happens again?"

"That's what I'm afraid of. I wasn't able to pull you out as soon as you probably would've liked. From my perspective, the whole thing only lasted five seconds for me. Your pulse was skyrocketing and your body started to shake into a seizure. For you, it seemed longer than that."

I was now starting to have regrets. Maybe this wasn't the best idea. On the other hand, I wouldn't have any answers to the questions I had. I still wouldn't know who that boy was in the photo next to me. I wouldn't have any leads on even who my father was. If the Caduceus could resurface old memories of a kid I had no recollection of, I didn't see any reason why it couldn't give me some insight to my father or a plethora of other things.

"What if I told you that what I saw could possibly give me an answer to a traumatic childhood event?" I said.

There was another brief silence between the two of us.

"Well, then I would say... I believe you," Jennifer replied. *"I would believe you one-hundred percent. I would then say to that, it may not be wise to pick at certain dormant memories that haven't been revisited in a while. Stepping into these old traumatic events can be a lot like stepping through a minefield. You don't know what memories you might resurface that were better left untouched, and it may be something you intentionally repressed long ago as a defense mechanism. I'm not saying this because you don't deserve to know, but maybe, your brain did this because it's best for you not to remember."*

I couldn't just brush off something like this. There was blood, lots of fucking blood in that room. That wasn't a mistake. That was real.

"How about, as a friend, can I trust you to make sure nothing bad happens to me up there?" I asked.

"Travis, I'm just a doctor part of the team here hosting your case study," Jennifer said. *"I mean, you seem like a decent guy, but outside of this we hardly know each other."*

"Yeah, but I've trusted you with the care of my brain thus far, and I'd say that's a heavy burden, wouldn't you?"

I didn't hear her say anything for a moment, but I could tell she was probably smiling or at least held a smirk. *"Fair enough. Alright, as a friend, you have my word. Just… be careful."*

I smiled. "I will."

And with that, I was on my own. Well, sort of. Jennifer may still be with me in a way, but what's to stop the same thing from happening last time where that would become obsolete? I'd beg and scream for her to let me out, but she wouldn't hear a single word…

◆◆◆

I focused hard on the word 'dandelion' again, closing my eyes, giving it about five seconds as usual. But I was afraid of what I knew for certain would show again. The screams. The blood. The bone-chilling fear I felt when I was there. No turning back now. I already started. And then, I opened my eyes.

To my disbelief (and I should also say to my relief), I wasn't in the party room again. Instead, I was in a bedroom of some sort. A bit like with Aunt Deborah's house, it was sort of incomplete and vague. But from what I could tell, it was a girl's bedroom. The walls were painted in a light rose pink, and there was a crochet oval-shaped rug in the middle of the room, patterned with white and hot pink rings shrinking closer to the center. A dresser and mirror stood against the wall adjacent to the door, and there were what I assumed to be makeup accessories such as lipstick and other sorts of brightly-colored items. But like with the memory of Aunt Deborah's, it was hard to really tell what exactly the items were, only the basic outline or shapes of what made sense in my mind.

The thing that really stood out in the room, and basically gave away the entire era was the box-shaped Panasonic CRT TV propped on top of a small pink wooden stand just inches off the ground.

The TV wasn't too big, about 24-by-24 inches, but noticeably outdated. It even had knob configurations and the speaker on the right side like many of the old ones did, to where it practically – almost laughably - looked like a microwave.

A bed was propped in the corner of the room with pink sheets and a white wooden board and frame, but that was all. No other details could be deciphered from my end. There were other things as well in the room that made it 'complete,' but I couldn't really interpret them any better than last time. Objects just sort of existed, and I couldn't focus, or rather remember enough to know what they were.

"Travis, just let me know if you need anything, okay?" Jennifer's voice blasted through my ear, which made me jump.

"Thanks," I said, embarrassed at myself from getting so spooked.

I wondered if this was another childhood memory. Things in this room felt similar to how they did in Aunt Deborah's, where the decor and setup seems outdated and very specific to the time period, specifically the 90s or early 2000s. It would make the most sense. This was another one of those memories where it was both obscure yet oddly familiar.

Then I heard thumping from the closet. I jerked my head in the direction, and froze with fear. It wasn't the party room, but yet I found myself with another reason to be scared.

You don't have to see anything you don't want to, I told myself in my head, and repeated it. But, what if I needed to?

I eased over to the door and reached out my arm for the knob. I heard more noise from inside the closet, telling me that someone, or something, was in there. As I got closer, I realized that I was now hearing voices from inside the closet. Small voices, like that of a child, and also what I swore was giggling. I held my breath, bracing for whatever might be on the other side.

Once I grasped the knob, I turned, and as I pulled the door not even entirely open, a small child came running out past me and out of the room.

I fell back against the wall beside me, catching myself. *What the hell?* I thought. But thankfully I got a glimpse of the boy as he ran by for the split second he was there in my face. It was him. Same one from the birthday party. I guess the trigger word worked after all, even if it didn't lead me to the same place.

I needed to go after him. He was the only person I'd seen in the Caduceus, aside from the figure that snatched him away. I don't know how, but maybe if I could talk to him…

No, that's not how it works, I don't think. The Caduceus goes off of memories that already occurred, not the imagination to make new ones. Making conversation would be virtually impossible, I'd imagine. At least that's how I remembered it in my mind. I could be wrong. But I had to try something.

I ran after him, and found myself in a hallway covered in the same old floral-patterned wallpaper everyone's grandmother seemed to have back in the day. Suddenly, the lighting was different. It was now a yellow-orange radiance coming from the light on the ceiling above. The floor was also carpeted, and across the hall from where I stood were white shuttered closet doors. Something in me just knew that's where the kid was hiding this time. I don't know why I was playing hide-and-go-seek with the rascal, but I didn't have the time.

I went towards the closet and swung open the doors. There he was, sitting down with a goofy smile and laugh as if we were still playing and that I caught him in the act.

"Who are you?" I asked.

He suddenly stopped laughing, and the cheerful demeanor on his face transformed into fear. But not at me, I don't think. He seemed to be looking *past* me. Then he let out a hair-raising scream.

I turned behind me to see what it was, and that same innate fear from before in the party room memory had returned. Across the hall stood a darkly dressed figure of some sort. The contrast from the end of the hall where they were standing and where we were likened to a blackhole eating all light that surrounded it. But I couldn't see their face, as it was too dark.

I felt the boy hug around my legs behind me for protection, as if he knew me. As if we'd been through something like this before…

I put my arm over him to shield him.

"He's getting closer!" the boy cried.

After that, I noticed that the figure was indeed moving closer to us, though, not with a steady walk, but an unusual shuffling of his feet inching forward towards us in an uncanny manner, like a stop-motion effect.

There was another room next to us, across from the other girl's bedroom I found myself in earlier.

"Here, go in here!" I pointed, keeping him shielded with my arm.

We both ran across into the other room as I shut the door behind us, locking it. This one was vastly different in both decor and overall theme. I could tell from first glance that it was a boy's room, the complete opposite of the other one I ended up in the first time.

There was a blue race car bed, black or perhaps navy blue-painted walls, an open toybox in the corner of the room with other sorts of toys and obscure items scattered across the floors that I was likely to forget in a matter of seconds, and peculiarly enough, an art painting on the door, likely from that of a kindergartener from the painted handprints and the style. However, there was no closet, and with the layout and design of the bed, there was no good spot for hiding.

Three small knocks sounded at the door. Pounding would have proved more comforting compared to the terrifyingly calm, tempered knocking of the pursuer on the other side. This couldn't be a memory, right? There was no way. This was a complete nightmare, no doubt about it. Either the machine was going haywire and fucking with my brain, or this really was something I decided to repress, rightfully so.

I took us both over to the race car bed and huddled in the corner, staring directly at the door.

"It's okay, just stay quiet," I whispered to the boy.

Again, I had no idea who this kid was, yet, for some strange reason, I had an innate response to do whatever I needed to protect him. But why? I didn't really think that mattered right now.

Three light knocks sounded from the door yet again, in a strangely playful manner.

As I looked to the door, I was simultaneously fixated on the painting that hung there. I took note of the handprints made out of paint. Green, yellow, and red, but mostly red. Red handprints. Was that what I saw before in the party room? When things went stark and downright creepy? The blood streaks scattered about the room…

Three knocks again. The boy whimpered out of fear.

Peering at the painting again, my vision started to shift focus elsewhere on the picture as well. Not just at the hands this time, but slightly above. It was that dried up squeeze paint that most children used for arts and crafts in primary school. Looking at the shape of the curves and corners, it made out a name, which, due to the Hub's vague image rendering, I had to focus extra hard to make out.

This time, the knocks turned into pounds, and there was jiggling at the door.

I needed to focus harder. I took a breath and kept my eyes keen on the painting like a hawk. I didn't even blink. I could determine that there were at least five letters, and there was no doubt in my mind that it was a name. It had to be. All I had so far was that it started with a 'T', and that there was a lowercase 'e' in there also.

"Tyler?" I uttered, taking a shot in the dark.

Suddenly, the boy looked at me in response, worry in his eyes. I was right. That's what his name was.

Tyler. But who was he to me? And then, to my horror, the sound of the latch releasing from the doorknob penetrated the previous dead silence of the room. Slowly, the door cracked open just an inch. What the fuck were they waiting for? I sure didn't have time to wait. I needed to leave, to be done with this simulation.

Quickly, I tightly shut my eyes and tried to think of a different place, hell, even the black void would go nicely right about now. I didn't know if I was going to lose the kid or not, but I couldn't take my chances staying here. It was just a memory, I told myself. None of this was real. I focused purely on returning to the black void, and didn't wait for five seconds to pass this time. I only did it for two, and forced my eyes open.

I didn't go anywhere, and the dark figure was now in my face. It reached its arms out and grabbed around my neck, beginning to strangle me. I could hear Tyler scream as my consciousness started to fade.

"J-Jennifer," I struggled to say.

•••

Thankfully, she heard me. Or, at least saw that I was in distress from her end. A fish-eye lens view of plain white met my eyes, which was immediately jerked away as Jennifer removed the headset from me. She unhooked the Caduceus entirely and immediately handed me a readily prepared cup of coffee. I touched around my neck with my hands, realizing that nothing was strangling me after all. It was just like last time. The reality of it all taking place and in just a matter of seconds it was over just like that…

"Here," she said, to which I accepted the Styrofoam cup from her hand. "You were doing it again, and your heartbeat was higher than last time, I think."

I took sips of the coffee, and when I realized it wasn't that hot, began gulping it down.

"My notes are gonna look great, but at the cost of you almost dying on me every time, I don't really think that's worth it," she added. I swallowed a sip of coffee, then set it aside. "This is serious stuff. You're the first person for us to be venturing in unknown territory like this, and I don't know what might be the right or wrong move to make because it's not something we're prepared for. What we're doing right now is playing with fire."

"I know his name," I said.

"What?"

"His name. The kid's name. I know his name now... it worked."

I still didn't have any leads on who my father was, but at least this was enough to go off of. I hope so, anyways.

•••

In the modern age of tech, it's easier than ever to find someone you're looking for, including those that were long forgotten from your past. Old classmates you went to school with, teachers, even people that are friends with *your* friends. You'll always be amazed by how big your network of associates really is once you start to dissect it... so why couldn't I find who this Tyler kid was?

I checked all my mutual friends' lists on all my social media platforms and still came up with nothing. I looked up the old elementary school I used to attend, tried searching through their site to maybe trace and hunt down any old yearbooks or photos that might give me some sort of clue, but nothing went back any further than 2018.

Come to think of it, what was I really searching for? I didn't even know which grade to start looking at. Could've been first grade, second grade, hell, pre-k even.

Suddenly, a notification on my phone popped up. It was for a calendar reminder. My Aunt Deborah's birthday was coming up, and I promised myself I'd get her a gift. Shit.

I decided I would pause for now and focus on finding her a gift really quick. Should I have pushed the notification much earlier to plan accordingly? Absolutely, but the past couple of weeks haven't exactly been the most conventional, and being punctual was the least of my worries.

Now I had to think of what gift would be the most suitable for her. Cooking utensils? She loved to cook, just like my mom. Jewelry? Yeah, that was always an easy one to settle for. She loved pearl necklaces, and I found one online that I was certain she'd adore. It didn't matter if it was cheap or not. For her, it was the appearance that mattered.

I put in my card information, billing address (which was still my mom's current address), and all the usual details, and received a 'Thank you!' message shortly after that popped up saying that my order should ship soon. A feeling of relief came over me once it was done, as I could now check that off my to-do list. Back to work.

However, as I was beginning to zone back into my research, another notification caused my phone to vibrate, distracting me again. Smacking my mouth, irritated, I grabbed and opened my phone once again. Turns out it was an e-mail notification from the site I just purchased the necklace from. For now, I just read the subject text, sliding the dropdown menu over to where I could read it. It read, "Issue with Purchase." Confused, I tapped on the message to open it.

From what the message read, the card was supposedly declined due to reasons unspecified. I rolled my eyes. Sometimes it was just a matter of the vendor not being able to process cards with certain banks, which was probably the case again, but just to be sure I went ahead and checked all the details I'd inputted.

Name. Check.

Card number. Check.

Expiration date. Check

Security code. Check

Address… wait a minute.

I read the exact address I'd put in.

4747 Lakeville Rd

It was akin to looking at something done the next day after a long night of incessant drinking (which for sure didn't happen *last* night). I didn't even recognize the address I typed in. Was I just out of it when I typed it, or just really tired? Any other time that would make some sort of sense, but this address was entirely foreign to me. It's not like I was only off by a number or misspelled a word in the line. The entire line was off. Then I looked down to what I put for the city and state. I shook my head in bewilderment.

Apopka, Florida.

It was all too specific...

I went ahead and searched the address. Low-and-behold, it was real. I switched to the satellite street-view so that I could see it for myself. From where it put me, I was in front of a small house in a neighborhood surrounded by other similar suburban homes.

That feeling came back again. The one I'd been experiencing since this whole thing started, a creeping sensation picking at the back of my brain, suggesting that the image of the house was in some way, unbeknownst to me, familiar. I knew it wasn't an accident now.

I fixed the issue and re-sent the proper information this time and then got back to the other matter at hand. I pulled up the page I had still open on my phone with the street-view of the house and just stared at it for a while. Why was it so nostalgic to me? I hadn't even known the place... had I?

I rotated the map to get a view of other houses and the streets in the neighborhood. Right then and there, it all hit me at once. Everything about the street. From the sidewalk. The grass. The fences. The other houses lined up across each other.

It's everything I'd seen back in the Hub, triggered by the word 'bicycle.' It took me up until now to realize that the Caduceus was able to resurface another memory I had no recollection of. The picture I'd found in my mom's attic of me riding my bicycle when I was small had the same background. It was so long ago, I figured it was just a far-gone memory that'd slipped my mind, and since I'd found the picture about a week ago, my subconscious chose to latch onto it. Because it was apparent to me now. But clearly, there was more to it. Somehow, I managed to remember the address to the same street with no explanation whatsoever.

Taking this newfound information, I went ahead and searched with the keywords "tyler" and "apopka". It was a shot in the dark. I had no idea if the connection between 'Tyler' and myself was at all related to the town. Just as I was about to hit search, I stopped myself.

Really, Travis? I thought. Who knows how many Tylers might pop up on any people finder site or white pages? I'd be at this shit for hours or even days. For all I know, 'Tyler' most likely doesn't live there anymore. If he did, it'd still be a while before I could maybe track him down. Regardless, I went ahead and hit the search option. I wasn't expecting to get anywhere from that, anyways. But then one of the links that popped up in the search results caught my attention.

'Kidnapped 7-year-old Florida boy found after…'

And that was all that the text could fit on the line before clicking on it to read the rest. The preview text detailed the article dating back to April 26, 2001. Just three days after my birthday. I felt goosebumps rising on my skin. I followed the link to read more. The local news station covered the story detailing everything.

Tyler Brigham.

"Oh shit," I whispered to myself.

That was his name. I finally found him.

I read everything. It started when Tyler and another kid named Brian Jones went missing after a birthday party at the local movie theater. The birthday was held inside a party room reserved specifically for special events of the sort. Sometime around 8:41 in the night, Tyler's parents noticed that they hadn't seen Tyler for a period of the evening, and soon they began to grow concerned. Shortly after checking through the building and in the party room, one of the parents' bodies was found stabbed to death in the room, stuffed into a closet. Soon after, it was discovered that Brian was also missing. They asked the local theater staff if they'd seen their kids or if they saw anybody else who may have come through that looked suspicious, to which they were unable to confirm. They then notified the authorities and soon it became reported as a child abduction and murder.

Tyler was missing for three days until he was finally found after a couple reported to the police that a kid was by himself roaming a random neighborhood, asking around for his parents. The boy gave his name and address, which he thankfully knew from memory, matching the description. Apparently, Tyler said the man just let him go. Unfortunately, however, Tyler had no clue as to the man's name or face. He likely wore a mask or kept it concealed from him somehow. As for Brian, he remained missing and presumed to be still under captivity by the abductee or possibly set free elsewhere.

Or dead, I thought. I know it was wrong to think things like that, but...

It was an out-of-body experience to read. Like something in an alternate reality apart from my own. The Caduceus checks out. Thus far, it told no lies.

The parent's body that was found in the party room. That would explain the blood I'd seen in the Hub. I guess it wasn't from red paint. Perhaps my brain had an issue distinguishing the two things from one another at the time. And the movie theater. That would also explain why I saw a theater lobby in one of the memories as well. And the screams. Tyler's screams…

Even the picture of Tyler that was shown in the article resembled his face in the one I had saved in my phone. I compared the photo of him next to me blowing out my birthday candles and the one on the screen, and it was an exact match. That was the Tyler I supposedly knew.. and then I recalled my mom's reaction when I first showed her the picture after finding it in the attic.

"I don't remember," she had said. I saw through the lie then, and now I have clear-cut evidence that confirmed it.

I guess Tyler was someone I knew, maybe even a friend of mine. I don't know. But why didn't I know? How could I forget something like that? Experiencing something like that at such a young age (hell, at any age), I'd be reminded of that night every year-round, I'd think.

But even more pressing... why did my mom lie to me?

◆ ◆ ◆

I found myself driving miles away from Austin, Texas, and all the way to a small community in Savannah, Georgia. I was still on holiday break for a couple more days, and if I drive fast enough without getting pulled over, I could be back in a timely manner before class was in session again. My destination? Tyler.

I finally tracked him down with enough clues to point me in the right direction to a rec center where he worked. How did I know it was 100-percent him? Honest to God, I was thorough. Made sure there weren't any possible holes in my search. Narrowed it down to about two other possible suspects. And hey, if it wasn't him, then I'd just search for the other two. I didn't mind cross-country drives. But I was certain it was him.

I didn't give him a heads up that I was arriving. I didn't even know if he'd be working when I eventually did show up. That's fine. I'd wait. I'd rather surprise him and not give him any time to possibly plan my arrival, as I'm not too sure what my history with this guy was. Best to remain low-key for this situation.

Nature here was quite different, I noticed. Moss hanging from oak trees varying in sizes from small to large like tentacles from the ground. Low-built height structures and homes that stood for decades. Large spaces of luscious green grass around nearly every neighborhood block. It was different, but pleasantly so.

The rec center building from what I could tell was built years ago, with a slightly faded, decrepit infrastructure that'd seen its fair share of days. I stared at the building for what seemed like hours, sitting in the parking lot in my car, just pondering. Was I just wasting my time driving all the way out here? Was I way over my head? His picture matched the one I had from us when we were kids. Sure, he'd aged since then by nearly two decades, but I knew it was him. I don't know how, but I just did.

When I walked inside, I instantly took in the refreshing air of the A/C and noticed the sofas, coffee table, and TV set up in the lounging area, as well as a couple of other gaming consoles, but I didn't see anyone here. Ahead of me was the front desk, also vacant. I was starting to think nobody was here at all, but then again, the door was open, and the hours said otherwise.

There was a bell sitting at the counter of the front desk, and shakingly, gave it a ring.

I waited for about 15 to 20 seconds, and in between that time stood nervously. What was I supposed to expect? And what was I to say?

I gave it another ring.

I stood there awkwardly again some more. My heartbeat anxiously pounded within my chest, growing faster with each passing second. I could just leave right now, I thought, as I turned away from the desk, facing out the window from the front door. I could leave right now and forget this even happened, just drive all the way back to Austin and it'll have been a wasted trip in hopes of some attempt at self-discovery-

"Hello," a voice sounded from behind the desk.

And for that brief moment, my heart stopped. Timidly, I turned to face who it was. God almighty, it was him. In the flesh. Tyler, though the same age as me, and certainly good-looking in his own right, looked more tired and beat by life than I did. Surely, we chose different paths after growing up together (whatever that meant).

"Can I help you?" Tyler added.

"Hi," I said. "Um, are you Tyler Brigham?"

I saw the perplexed look on his face. "Who's asking?" he awkwardly answered.

I knew there was no turning back now. I'd made it this far, dammit.

"I know this is a bit awkward and out of the blue," I said, "and I don't know if you remember me or not, but... I'm Travis... I think we grew up together."

Tyler tilted his head with a lost look. "Travis?" he said.

I nodded. "Do you remember me?" I nervously asked.

From reading his face, still nothing.

"I'm sorry, I'm not sure I do," Tyler said.

I tried again. "Do you remember back in Florida? The birthday party? It was *my* birthday, and you and a bunch of other kids were there, and..." I hesitated.

I knew digging up something so traumatic maybe wasn't the most appropriate nor best idea. That's all I'd been doing the past couple of weeks, though.

"*Your* birthday?" Tyler quietly said. My throat tightened, and I nodded. "... Brian?" he said.

◆◆◆

He agreed to speak with me later once he got off work at the center, which was just a couple of hours after I managed to run into him, where we could then discuss things further. The place we were meeting at was a nice quiet park surrounded by mossy trees and neatly-trimmed grass. A paved trail slithered throughout the establishment with a park bench that stood on the side with the perfect breathtaking view of the nature that surrounded it. Right now, its occupant was Tyler as he sat there with his leg shaking steadily up and down as I approached. Could he be just as anxious to see me as I was with him?

Taking notice of me headed his way, he turned his head to face me and stood from the bench. I stopped several feet in front of him on his edge of the bench.

"Wanna sit?" he asked.

I nodded. "Sure."

I took a seat next to him, evenly distanced, and began to awkwardly look off to the ground, as he did, falling into a worried state of consciousness as my mind raced aimlessly, wondering which of us was going to start first. He seemed like a decent guy, he really did. But still, I knew somewhere within Tyler that he was hiding something. Not deception per se, but rather *pain*.

"How did you find me?" he started.

I swallowed nervously. "I tracked you through social media," I answered honestly. "And other methods. Internet, mostly."

He nodded. "Sounds about right. I'm just surprised. I haven't seen you in years. Not since…"

I attentively turned to face him now. "Since what?" I asked.

I could see he was nervous, too. "Since your seventh birthday," he answered.

I knew that was the answer, but I needed it to come from his mouth. I felt a tightening sensation in my chest. He remembered. Not only did he remember me, but he remembered very well that day what we were doing and what it was for. And he specifically remembered that it was my *seventh* birthday. Not my sixth, not my eighth.

"What do you remember?" I asked. "From that day?"

He looked at me now. "Don't *you*?" he replied.

I looked him dead in the eye and shook my head. "Tyler, I don't remember anything. I don't know why, but I just don't. But I'm starting to."

Utter disbelief drew all over his face as if what I said was ludicrous.

"Well," he started, "I can't say I blame you for it."

"What do you mean?"

He shot another muddled glance at me, looking off to the side and back.

"Do you really not remember?" he said. "Like, not a single thing?" I fearfully shook my head. He scoffed, with slight irritation in his tone, "What made you change your mind?"

At this point, it'd be best to come clean and just tell it all, no matter how ludicrous it might sound.

"I partook in this experiment," I began. "This sort of group study on this device they call the Caduceus. It's worn like a headset that syncs to your brain. It's supposed to be a way to bridge the gap between our conscious and subconscious minds, allowing you to see old or even recent memories, or, at least vague sort of remnants of the memory or thought. It's more vivid than dreaming could ever be, it's... like nothing I've ever seen before. I see all sorts of shapes, objects, buildings, landscapes, places. In the end, they all point to specific moments from your life that happened. Things you'd simply forgotten about, or didn't realize were there before. It's incredible, really, but..."

I started to trail off. Tyler watched me attentively, awaiting my next important piece of detail. I kept it going. I had to know.

"Up until this point, I thought I had a pretty normal life. I passed every grade, graduated high school, I'm studying Drama - something I still haven't told my mom about me switching degrees - and, you know, I just felt like an average guy living an average life, and I was okay with that. But when I look back on my childhood, the memories I had about growing up... I realize I don't have many at all. I don't even remember what it was like. Doing paintings in class. Recess. Naptime. Playing with toys - I mean, I don't recall having any growing up. I couldn't remember even if I tried. My old teachers, from kindergarten or first grade… everything's a blur to me before second grade. I can't even recall the old neighborhood I grew up in. I… I can't even remember my own dad." Tyler remained silent, just listened. "I've never felt so… *abnormal* in my life up until now."

A glint of cognizance emerged in Tyler's eyes. "You really don't remember," he whispered.

"I don't know why," I said. "There's just remnants of things. I was in a bedroom, a girl's room. There was a bulky TV on top of a pink stand, a dresser with all sorts of nail polish and random stuff with a big mirror, and a circular rug…"

"Clarissa's room," Tyler said.

"Huh?"

"My sister Clarissa? You're talking about her room?"

I shrugged. "I don't know who that is."

"She used to kick us out all the time whenever you and I went snooping through her things. We were annoying little shits. We used to play hide-and-go-seek all the time at my place. I'd always choose her room because you knew not to go in there and it'd be the last place I'd expect you to look."

Hide-and-go-seek. Just as we did in the Hub.

"You picked the closet, didn't you?" I asked.

Tyler nodded. "Yeah. Yeah, I totally did. Or sometimes under the bed."

"You also had a painting of your name on your door. Your walls were painted dark blue, I think, and your bed was a blue race car."

Now he started to look a little more upbeat and loosened up.

"I sure did," he said. "I didn't even remember that. It's just been that long."

"I only know this because everything I'd seen in the Caduceus was very recent. Before any of this, those memories might as well have been nonexistent to me. I would've never known. All I know is that you were kidnapped, being taken away by some figure, and there being blood in the party room where we had my birthday. And some other kid with you, I think, some kid named-"

And once again, I couldn't speak. My throat clenched and my chest tightened like a locked cage.

"You called me Brian earlier," I quietly said. "That was the kid that the news said was also…"

I couldn't even finish my sentence. A sick sensation grew in my gut. If I said anything else I was afraid it might travel up to my throat.

The vision came back of Tyler being dragged away by the figure behind the door, except the memory was a bit different this time. Instead, it was *me* on the other end of that door. *I* was being taken. It was like a bad broken record I couldn't get out of my head and would just pop up at any given moment.

•••

I drove miles and hours through heavy rain all the way back to my mom's place. I don't even remember stopping to rest. Only stopped to get gas when I needed it and kept going. I had to have stopped, that was a long-ass drive from Georgia back to Texas. Yet, I didn't recall...

What I did remember, however, was more images flooding my mind. Liminal spaces. That's what Jennifer called them. Empty spaces of areas that in the back of my mind, I feel I visited at some point in my life, yet, I had no way to be certain. Empty malls, playgrounds, random corridors that led to nowhere... they crossed the barrier between nostalgia and unfamiliarity all at once.

It's all I could think of while I traveled on the interstate. My body was in autopilot mode as I took hold of the wheel, but my mind was racing. New neural pathways opened that had never been opened before, or rather, opening for the first time in years of lying dormant.

•••

When I finally did make it back to the house, I saw the lights were on, giving away that she was home. I rang the doorbell and she answered to find her son standing there drenched in a light coat that hardly did the job. Her face looked delighted to see me, and she reached her arms out for a hug, but I raised my hand. She drew back, confused, and I simply stepped inside, walking past her.

I took a seat at the kitchen table where my back turned to her. My silent treatment was probably scaring her, no doubt. I heard the sound of her footsteps getting closer as she approached me, and then she made it over to my side, where she stood looking down at me with a worried expression.

"You okay, hon?" she said.

I remained silent for a moment. I didn't even want to look at her.

"I spoke to Tyler," I said.

My mother stirred. "You what?"

I slowly turned my head to face her with a cold stare in my eyes. From my mother's own expression, I knew it frightened her.

"Why didn't you tell me I was kidnapped?" I bluntly asked.

••

Everything was quiet in the house. Nevertheless, the tension was palpable. We stared at each other for an indelible moment in time I could never take back. One of us would have to speak first to break the silence. But I waited patiently. Not out of respect, but because it'd be in my mother's best interest to do so...

"Hon..." she started, her voice shaky. "Where is this coming from? Who have you been talking to-

"If you lie to me one more time, I'm never speaking to you again," I snapped.

Dismay noticeably rose from her gut to her throat and onto her face..

"Who told you?" was all she could muster.

"So it's true?" I remarked. "You admit it."

Her face was flushed with red as she began to awkwardly pace, fiddling with her necklace.

"I wondered why you acted so strange when I showed you that picture," I continued. "The one from my seventh birthday. Usually, a mother doesn't forget those types of things, especially one of an only child."

"W-Where did you-" my mom stammered, struggling to speak. I'd never seen her so helpless, so vulnerable. It was almost heartbreaking to watch... *almost*.

"No, answer me, Ma. Why did you lie to me?!" I interrupted. "I never lied to you once! I was always a good kid, always made it home before the streetlights came on, never snuck out to a party - didn't get in any sort of trouble growing up - well shit, at least that's what I thought, don't really have a clue anymore, but what do I fucking know, right?"

"Travis-"

"My name's what, Brian? Is that even true?"

"Honey, please-"

"Are you even my real mother-"

"Yes!" she cried. "Yes, I'm your real mother…" Her eyes filled with tears now. "Yes… it's true. All of it."

But that still didn't satisfy me. There was so much more she knew that hadn't been told, and I was gonna get everything out of her tonight.

I scoffed. "I don't even know the *half* of it, Ma. I've been having crazy dreams - nightmares - and every day I have more and more moments where I just suddenly remember something I didn't know before.

I've learned more about myself these past couple weeks than I have my entire life!"

"It's that thing you've been using, isn't it?" my mother asked. "That machine or whatever. I knew I had a reason to be worried about you using that thing-

"Why, though? Why would you keep something like that from me?!"

"For your own good, goddammit! You think I wanted to remind you of something like that - do you think *I* wanted to be reminded?"

"Oh, because it's about you, right? That's what this is? You protecting yourself and me to just 'deal with it'?"

"No, baby, that's not what this is about." She stepped over to me, kneeled on one knee and gently cupped my hands. "I wanted to protect *you*. You've always been my number one priority. It's always been about you. Baby, you have to know that. You have to."

With spite, I gave her a look that made her withdraw, jerking my hands away from hers.

"Oh, *I* have to know that?" I mocked. "I don't know anything, Ma. Up until now I didn't even know I had a best friend growing up, and that we were both kidnapped by the same guy."

She had a lump in her throat, but swallowed and got on with it. She had to.

"Travis, honey, I'm going to tell you everything. Okay? I promise…"

"'Travis'…" I scoffed, shaking my head. "Why'd you move those boxes in the attic?" I asked.

"I-I want to risk you seeing anything else in them that might…"

She stammered trying to find the words. "Might what?" I argued impatiently.

"I don't know, might make you remember," she answered.

"Remember what?! The kidnapping? The party?"

Tears rolled down her cheeks. "All of it. All of it…"

There was a brief silence. My mother walked away into the kitchen to contain herself, wiping away her tears.

Then I asked the question, "Where's my dad really?"

She then came back towards the table and took a seat across from me.

"It was your seventh birthday," she began. "You said you wanted a big party with all your friends from the neighborhood and school. Including Tyler. Especially Tyler. Tyler was your best friend when you two were little. Same age, same hobbies, same personalities. You two did everything together. Shoot, I think his mom and myself had to even come up with a schedule as to when you two could have free time with each other to go play outside, or either you hang out at his house or vice versa. The both of you were inseparable..."

And yet, I knew. I felt the same way when I first saw him in the Caduceus, the way I just instinctively felt that I'd met him before. Like a long-lost friend from juvenescence.

She continued. "Your father and I decided to plan your birthday at the local movie theater, then we'd go back to our place for a couple others to hang out in the backyard to play games before their parents sent them home. Tyler, a couple other kids from the neighborhood, some of your classmates - everyone was there."

My father... the man I couldn't remember for the life of me.

"The night went well. We went to go see *Spy Kids*, since that was the only real kids movie that was out then at the time still playing. Some of the kids had already seen it, but that was fine. It was a party after all. They were just glad to be there."

She paused for a moment to recollect her thoughts.

"Everything was well up until the point where..."

She hesitated. But I knew what she was going to say.

"The murder," I answered for her.

She nodded.

"Sasha was a single mother," my mom went on. "Derrick and Melissa were her only children. I urged her to go and bring them to the party. Really urged her. Told her it would be great for the kids. And I regret that decision every day."

That was the only time I felt any sort of empathy for her at this moment.

"One of the parents and other kids found her body," she continued. "There was screaming - *lots* of screaming. Everything had turned into chaos. Your father and I knew the night had been ruined, but at least we could do our best to comfort you and reassure you that things were going to be all right." Her voice began to break again, and more tears formed. "Of the few things I felt I could do at the time, at least I had *that*. The power to comfort and reassure you. Tell you what had happened in the best possible way I could. But… we couldn't find you. I looked everywhere. We searched up and down the theater in every possible place, thinking you may have hidden in fear or something." She shook her head, wiping her tears. "We couldn't find you, baby. You or Tyler. We didn't sleep for days. I was so exhausted I nearly passed out throughout the day just working with the police and search team around the clock. I couldn't even stand up by myself at one point."

I'd seen my mother cry more than I ever had before. All the other times were from moments of joy, like my graduation and such. But never of anguish. Never of despair. It was only a matter of time before the tears began to form from my own eyes.

"That's why you changed my name," I said. "So that we could move on?"

She nodded, sniffling and wiping away more tears.

"For your protection. For the two of us."

"The two of us? What about my dad?"

My mom shook her head.

"As hard as it may seem to believe, honey, your dad's more a part of your life than you may realize," she said.

I didn't feel any specific type of way towards the statement. I neither loved or nor hated my father, due to the simple fact that he didn't exist to me. It'd already been accepted as a way of life.

"What happened?" I asked. "Why did he leave?"

My mother nervously twiddled her thumbs, which told me that everything she'd said so far wasn't even the half of it. I swallowed, feeling another lump grow in my throat.

"Your dad was a neurosurgeon," she said. "He performed countless procedures and operations throughout his career – heck, I don't even know to what extent, it wasn't my line of work. But I do know that he was good at it. And... he had connections in the field with more... off-the-book operations."

I asked what that could possibly mean with the nonverbal expression on my face.

"Basically, your father knew how to pull some strings to get any sort of procedure done for those only with a specific 'need-to-know,'" she explained. "Was it legal? Shit no, but that was out of the question."

"Why can't I remember?" I asked in a low, scared whisper.

She took in a deep breath before proceeding to tell, this all being much harder for her than for me, it seemed.

"You were gone for two weeks," she blurted. "Two weeks. That son of a bitch had my baby for two whole weeks." The tears came back, but she pressed through. "Do you realize what a miracle it is that you're alive? Everyone thought you were going to be another number, just another victim of child abduction. Me and your father couldn't afford that. We couldn't afford to give up even when everyone else did. And I knew. I knew what some of them were thinking. I knew that they thought that my baby was a goner and a lost cause. I knew that… and they could fuck off."

I got up from the table and began to pace about.

"When we finally did get you back… you weren't the same, honey," she continued. "You weren't the same innocent sweet boy we remembered. You'd changed. Understandably so, you had changed. Whatever he did to you… whatever you saw… it changed you so much."

Flashes of different images played through my mind again like a broken record. An empty play room that distorted into a bare, four-wall cement block with a small chair and table propped in the corner covered in toy blocks, as well as a mini slide and playground setup on the opposite end. And of all things, the dark figure. The man. He was always there.

"What did my dad do?" I asked. Innately, though, I think I already knew the answer.

"Like I said," my mom started again, "Your dad knew how to pull some strings. Him and I talked for a very long time. Thought hard about the decision we were about to make. All the pros and cons were elaborated. At first I said no. Hell no. I didn't stop asking any questions until I was certain it would be fine."

I stopped pacing, standing completely still, and looked at my mom hard in the face.

"The two of you had my memory wiped," I said for her.

She confirmed with a nod. "Selective memory suppression. It was the safest way to go. There's a lot of 'way out there' procedures that aren't open to the public, aside from lobotomy. No way in hell were we going to do anything *that* severe. Any other procedure would be asking us to give permission to have neurons and synapses removed from your brain. There's always the risk of impaired function in other aspects if you're not careful, though. And things could always develop later. So, we decided on suppressing the memory as much as possible. Like pushing it back down into the furthest reaches of your memory without actually erasing the memory. That was the catch."

And the Caduceus had awakened everything again, I came to the conclusion, setting off a chain of events.

"There was no guarantee that you wouldn't have the slight off-chance of remembering," my mother went on. "There was always that possibility. So… for the sake of making sure there was no chance for him to trigger any memories of your time with your captor, your father and I agreed for him to not be in your life." The words cut deeper than I expected. For someone I had no feelings for, it hurt no less to hear. "For the first couple of weeks when you were back," – she shook her head – "I don't know, it was as if his presence, his appearance alone set you off. Like you were afraid to even be around your dad. It was just…"

She took a moment again to recollect herself.

"He left so that I wouldn't be reminded of the man," I said, understanding now. My mother nodded.

"I wished I could've given you the childhood every kid deserves," she said through muddled eyes. "Every kid deserves love and joy from a young age. So once that was taken from you, we did what we thought was best for you. We had a chance to start over for you. You had a chance at a normal life again. One where you didn't have this... chip on your shoulder. One where you wouldn't have nightmares or the trauma of trying to fit in with the rest of your peers and go about your regular life. We could finally give that to you again, and we did. All the people who probably talked amongst themselves or thought to themselves that our baby wouldn't be able to make it in life – you did! You graduated high school, went off to college, you're following your dreams now and decided to study drama. You did it, honey."

I looked at her again. "How did you know I switched degrees?" I asked her.

She smiled, shaking her head. "I'm your mother," she said. "I know."

At the cost of being privileged enough, though, I thought to myself. Tyler came to mind, and how his eyes appeared when I first saw him again back in Georgia, how beat they were. I understood why he looked that way now. As it would for any child to experience that at such a young age, it messed him up. The difference between seeing how he once was as a child to his adult persona was heartbreaking. And here I was, just living my life, going about my business with strings holding me back this whole time. Never once did I feel guilty about anything until now. Even with my second chance at life, I felt an undeniable surge of guilt.

"Did they ever find the man who took us?" I asked.

From my mom's nervous twiddling of her thumbs again, and the uncontrollable rise and descent of her chest, her body language said all.

No.

•••

At this hour of the night, I'd have to be completely out of my mind to accept any invitation for a late-night meet-up at a café, so I was surprised to see that Jennifer accepted my invitation at all. Seeing her outside of her lab coat attire was almost comical, as she was a completely different person entirely in a jacket and jeans.

She took a seat across from me at the table, sitting down her purse at her side.

"Hey," she said.

"Hey," I returned a less lively greeting.

"I got your voicemail. I was in the shower when you called, but I headed over as soon as I heard. What's up?"

I gazed through the window into the outside nightlife, noticing how the lights along various shops and buildings lit up from one another. From this angle, they didn't even look real to me. Rather, I saw them more as artificial designs, like the ones in the Hub. After all, that's what they were. Though, the more I opened my eyes to the things around me, everything began to seem that way.

"You know how when I was in the Hub, how everything had a common theme?" I spoke. "The stage. The set designs. How everything just felt theatrical? I think I get it now. It's not about how creative I am. It's not about how desperate my mind wants to be itself and pursue its dreams and express itself through theatrics. No..."

I shook my head, looking Jennifer right in the face. Her focus was attentive as always, but this time with a diffident edge.

"Imitation," I continued. "That's what it is. Everything I thought I knew about myself – *think* I know about myself – it's all a lie. It's just props, fancy lighting, smoke and mirrors. None of it's real."

"Travis, *this* is real," Jennifer spoke with conviction. "You and me sitting here. You being in college. You having these thoughts and coming to this understanding of yourself a little later than you maybe hoped. All of this is real."

I shook my head, letting out a small chortle. She almost sounded like my mother.

"That's not even my real name," I said. "I was born Brian Jones, not Travis Thompson. My own identity is a lie. As far as I knew, everything I ever did was built on a lie."

"Why do you believe it was a lie?" she asked. "Why do you feel lied to?"

She had no idea. She had no idea at all...

"Me and my long-forgotten best friend when we were kids... we were kidnapped at my birthday party. This was so many years ago. I'd just turned seven. And had it not been for the Caduceus, had it not been for me meeting you, I'da never known. Would've went my whole life without ever knowing that I was a completely different kid. It's just little things I never would've thought about. Like why I hate the color red. Despise it – just for no apparent reason. That's what I always thought. I just *hate* the color red. Now I know… the blood…

"And the way I never liked going to the movies. Especially if the theater lobby was red. As well as the seats. It had to be the right theater, if I *was* to go. I didn't think about these things before… I get it now."

Jennifer stayed silent, as she certainly realized right about now that there was no way around this. No mental tricks, no shortcuts around it, nothing to make the moment feel any less than what it was. She could only listen.

"I can't remember anything because that's the way my parents intended it to be," I continued. "They wiped my memory of it. Suppressed it. So far back that it might as well be nonexistent. And here I thought the Caduceus was truly groundbreaking. They gave me another chance, Jennifer. They gave me another shot at life again. To be a normal kid again."

Tyler's face popped up in my head again. Seeing him as a kid compared to now…

"But Tyler…" I began, my eyes wandering off. "Tyler remembers everything. Not a day goes by where he wishes he didn't have to."

My eyes wandered off from where we were sitting that I barely noticed Jennifer wiping a tear from her face.

"And he's still out there," I added. "That bastard is still out there doing this to someone else's kid. Or hell, maybe he's dead or retired, or whatever. But who knows how many kids he's done this to? Kids that weren't as lucky as me to not have to remember." I leaned forward to look Jennifer firmly in the face. "I have to go back in the Hub," I told her.

She scoffed. "Travis, you know I can't let you do that."

"Every time I do, I remember more," I argued. "I remember something new I didn't before. And I'm willing to bet I know what that motherfucker's face looks like."

She shook her head. "Both times you went in, you remember what happened?" she said. "You keep going at this rate, you might not come back."

I sighed, then pulled out the flash drive she'd given me before. "It's the only shot we have at identifying him. We can get him on record – get his face on screen. I can finally put him behind bars for him to rot."

"You're not understanding. It's not just a matter of you going into cardiac arrest. Each time I've sent you and other subjects into the Hub, there was always a limit in how much time you're allowed inside. It varies from person to person, but in our case, each time, our sessions were cut short due to – well, obviously, we know why. For some people, too much time inside the Hub can be… dangerous. Especially so for you. In just a short amount of time, you've used the Caduceus more than many others who've participated in the study. You've gone way past the allowed limit. Any more and… your brain will defend itself by any means necessary. When it feels threatened or overwhelmed – attacked - it can get so lost in the Hub, so lost in the simulation, the traumatic event, or, even the opposite, pleasant memory… it could put you in a vegetative state. It won't want to leave."

I knew she wasn't lying, and that only scared me just a bit more. But not enough.

"And if I don't do anything, then what? This guy just gets away scot-free," I shook my head furiously.

"You realize how much trouble I would get in if I helped you?" Jennifer noted.

"If you get caught," I added.

"Travis."

"I'm only asking you as a friend. Only as a friend. Help me catch this guy."

•••

Silence filled the empty halls and offices during this hour, as Jennifer and I remained the only occupants within the facility. She had the capabilities and appropriate access to run the lab herself as she booted up the Caduceus and attached the heart monitor to my wrist while I sat in the chair. Jennifer was risking her career for me. Everything had to count. I couldn't waste any time.

"Do I really have to ask if you've eaten anything in the past eight hours?" she said.

"Hmm," I scoffed.

She looked me in the eyes. "Do you know exactly what you're gonna do when you get in there?"

"Yes," I nodded.

"I'm assuming you don't need my help this time?"

"I wouldn't say that. I need you to make sure my heart doesn't stop."

"Oh, I'll be sure to stay on top of that. I don't need to go prison anytime soon."

"Thank you, Jennifer. Seriously."

"I'm only doing this as a friend. But the moment your vitals start fluctuating – your pulse, respiration drops, or dangerously increases – I'm pulling you out. No thoughts about it. Are we clear on that?"

I nodded, knowing good and well that she was serious. I had one shot.

Once everything was set up, Jennifer stood next to the computer, ready to start the countdown shortly.

"Travis?" she said to me.

"Yeah?"

"Be brave."

She launched the program, and the high-pitched whirring protruded into both of my ears. Jennifer then commenced the countdown.

"5… 4… 3… 2…"

Before she reached 'one,' I was standing in the black void of my subconscious yet again. The empty stage. I wasn't lost, though. I knew what I had to do.

"Jennifer?" I called out.

"*Yes? I'm here,*" she responded from elsewhere.

"Can you give me the word this time? To help guide me in the right path again?"

"The word?"

"Yes. The one that started all this mess."

There was a momentary silence before hearing her say, "Alright."

I closed my eyes and took in steady deep breaths, anticipating her voice to initiate the trigger word. I'd have to calm myself – be my own support system. Make sure I didn't hyperventilate or cause any sudden panic, otherwise Jennifer would cut this whole thing short. Rightfully so, of course. But I couldn't afford that.

And with that, her voice uttered the four syllables, "*Dandelion*."

In the center of some sort of indoor courtyard, around me were numerous house structures built into the walls like venues, small shops around the corner of a typical shopping center. But I wasn't standing in a mall, from what I could tell. More like the façade of an outside neighborhood, except inside, and with a peculiar sense, underground even. Buildings within a building. It was so empty, so quiet...

Each front porch of the different 'houses' set themselves apart from one another in color all the way to size and material. Some wooden, some brick. As I walked down a long, seemingly endless corridor, I peeked into every other home through the front windows, seeing that they each held their own unique interior. But they were empty. The only objects that I could perceive were the occasional chandeliers, stair railings in the ones with more than one level, and carpeted or sometimes plywood flooring. Each house told its own story. Yet, there were so many. How many houses had I been in to truly remember them all? My subconscious couldn't be making it up.

"*Travis, are you okay?*" Jennifer asked.

"Yeah, I'm still here," I responded. "I'm in some weird place. It's like a neighborhood inside of an underground mall or something. I don't understand."

"Do they still look like set designs?"

"Yeah, but more… I don't know, detailed. More precise."

I continued down the endless avenue of empty homes, glancing over my shoulder every other moment.

"Are you still taking notes?" I had to ask.

"*Only if it's okay with you? Off-the-book,*" Jennifer said. "*As of now, anyways.*"

"You have my utmost consent."

I then stumbled across a particular home with a brick red exterior, with a house number '4747.'

That was the one.

The door was left open. Taking another deep breath, preparing myself, I carefully approached the front porch, noticing a small table and two chairs in front of the window, and stepped inside the recreation of my childhood home.

As with my experience in Aunt Deborah's home, the Hub filled in every single detail to the brim. There was some furniture – a couch, armoire, artificial plants, the kitchen table directly ahead, parallel to the kitchen just to the side of it, and the sliding glass door to the backyard.

Astoundingly, there was sunlight seeping through the windows of the sliding door into the house, indicating that there was an outside after all, just not from the other end. Then I remembered, the Hub was strange like that. It defied usual laws of physics.

Exploring the house gave an odd sense of familiarity, as though I knew my way around just fine despite having not stepped foot into the place since forever ago. The giant CRT TV in the living room entertainment center showed its age, reminding me just how old I was compared to when we were living in the house.

When I entered the dining area, I noticed a small birthday cake that sat atop the table. I for sure didn't see it there before when I first stepped foot inside. As I got a closer look at it, I counted six candles sticking into the cake in a circular pattern, the words 'Happy Birthday Travis' transcribed into the surface with icing. This was the year before, I came to understand. This was exactly a year before the incident. Before my seventh birthday.

"I'm in my childhood home," I said to Jennifer. "In perfect detail. I remember…"

"*What do you see now?*" she asked.

"The kitchen. The living room. Everything. I can remember just where everything was like it was yesterday."

"*As you may already have noticed, Travis, every time you go into the Hub, old dormant neural pathways open back up, increasing each time.*"

"I remember more and more every time I go in," I acknowledged.

"*Yes.*"

The candles on the cake were lit, waiting to be blown out. As the birthday boy, I went ahead and did the honor. I watched as the smoke vanished into thin air. Was that a memory that I was seeing right now, I wondered? The strings of smoke floating? The smell of the candles being blown out? Or was it something my mind was consciously making up as we go? Could my mind really be capable of remembering every single thread of smoke dissolving into nothingness? I walked away to avoid being bothered more by the question.

Upstairs was my room. There wasn't much to it from what I saw. A bare carpeted room with just a small Batman-themed bed in the corner, a tiny table and chairs on the opposite side, and scattered toys onto the floor, each with their own indiscernible shape. Like with the other objects I'd seen through memories from the Hub, staring at the objects too hard might drive me crazy trying to pick out exactly what they were. Might've been blocks, might've been G.I. Joes, coloring books even. They were just toys, I had to tell myself. That's all. No need to pick out every detail.

Perhaps the reason my old room looked so bare now was due to it being such a distant memory. If my dad was truly a neurosurgeon, as my mother had told me, I have no doubt they could afford to put together my childhood dream bedroom.

I stepped over to the window and stared down at the sidewalk just outside the house. There he was, standing there peering back at me. The dark figure's face remained concealed from me as before, either from the trick of light or given that he was too far away. Even from the first encounter with him, however, I remembered that up close I was still unable to get a good look at his face. I began to contemplate, in a frightening suggestion, that this was all a waste of time. That there was no way I can be sure that I remember his face at all, if I'd even seen it. What if he wore a mask to protect his identity the whole time I was with him?

For two whole weeks?!

I had to have laid eyes upon his own at some point. He couldn't hide it from me forever, I figured. At some point he'd have to-

Suddenly, a stark realization had come over me. This wasn't a dream. This wasn't a work of my imagination to fill in the blanks. None of those things were possible in the Hub…

This was all real. An actual memory. Me standing here in my childhood home, staring down through the window, noticing the man watching me from afar… this was just a recap. Nothing was being influenced by a trick of the Caduceus controlling objects or people as though they were puppets. It could replicate things to the best of its ability by making a theme out of it – the 'imitation' of actual environments. But the events were all the same, just as real as they'd been years ago. And as I stood here staring back at the kidnapper, it all hit me at once.

Right here and right now, this was the moment I first met the man in black, not at the movie theater on the night of my birthday. He'd been watching me the whole time. A whole year prior – a crime in the making.

The dark figure began to move, headed directly towards the house. I watched as he disappeared from the view of the window and made his way to the front door.

I rushed outside of the room and into the hall. There was the bathroom directly ahead, the one I'd used all the time. It was specifically for me since it was also the closest to my room. I went inside and shut the door, turning on the light. In the reflection of the mirror stood not myself, but my younger six-year-old self. I couldn't be entirely sure, but it had to be around that age. It looked just like me, matching my every movement with my head and hands as I tested it.

This wasn't a memory. It couldn't be. It wasn't possible for things to act independently on their own, or so I thought.

"Can you talk to me?" I asked my younger self. The past 'me' in the mirror shyly nodded.

So I was wrong. I could communicate with my other self. But how? The memory with Tyler – the game of hide-and-go-seek – that wasn't a trick of the imagination, was it? It was an actual memory. It had to be. But when I called his name in the Hub, he responded to me in real time, as though he were actually there. I didn't quite understand...

"How do we stop him?" I asked.

But the kid in the reflection doubtfully shook his head.

"You can't," he quietly spoke. "If you don't do what he says... he'll punish us."

He'll punish us.

Just like it was yesterday, the memories came flooding back all at once, in the fraction of a second, and to my detriment, I fully understood what he'd meant by 'punish.' My worry and fear soon transformed into anger.

"He won't do it again," I promised. "Not to anyone. I need to catch him. Tell me, how do I catch him?"

"You have to play hide-and-go-seek," my younger self answered. "That's his favorite game."

I felt a sick twist in my stomach. God, is that what we did all those years ago? With Tyler?

"You have to count down from ten," myself in the mirror clarified. "Once you're ready, you have to say, 'Ready or not- "

"Here I come," I said with my reflection.

I knew exactly what the deal was. It'd be just like old times…

I stepped back from the mirror, rubbing my face and scratching my head as I braced myself. I took more steady deep breaths to stay calm, hoping that I hadn't gone into full shock by now on Jennifer's end. I hadn't heard from her in a bit, but I wasn't too worried this time.

I closed my eyes and prepared to start the game.

"10," I sounded off. "9… 8… 7… 6… 5… 4… 3… 2…" I took in one last deep breath before completing the countdown. "One! Ready or not… here I come."

•••

I opened the bathroom door and stepped into a different setting entirely. A wide curvy corridor with white walls and a carpeted floor with a design congruent to that of vintage arcades and movie theaters, the same as the movie theater that I'd been snatched from. Rainbow confetti-style art plastered randomly about in different parameters across the floor.

Before, I wouldn't have been able to even recognize this place. But I knew exactly where I was now. An old indoor children's amusement center my parents took me one time. I stepped cautiously through the windy path, closely monitoring every small blind spot I passed from each wide arc in the walls.

Running footsteps sounded from behind. I jerked my head back only to find no one there.

"*T... T-Travis,*" Jennifer's voice came into my ear, making me jump.

"Jennifer?" I responded.

"*Travis, can you hear me?*"

"Yes, just fine."

"*Where are you? Are you safe?*"

"I don't know about safe," I remarked as I continued down the wall, watching my back at the same time.

"*That's not funny.*"

It was comforting, though, knowing that she was here with me, in a since. Her voice alone kept me afloat.

"If I panic, if my heart starts running a hundred miles per hour, don't pull me out until I say so," I said.

"I know this isn't what you want to hear, Travis, but I can't do that," she firmly stated. *"I can't risk your life like that."*

"Jennifer, I have to see him. I have to."

"I know but- "

The transmission between her and I got cut off again, and all around me followed heavy silence.

"Shit," I muttered.

I heard more footsteps running ahead from out of my view. Swallowing nervously, I stepped over to the echoing sound, not having anything but my hands to defend myself with. When I reached around the corner of the hall towards the source of the noise, I was met with the end of the hall and two wide purple double doors. They were cartoonishly structured in shape and size, almost like something out of a *Candy Land* set.

Entering through the other side, a huge space of various playsets, ranging from miniature houses, castles, a small kitchen set, fun-sized animals such as tortoises and horses, trampolines, bounce houses, monkey bars, and an array of many more objects I couldn't process all at once. Some of them I remembered from when my parents brought me here years ago.

I stepped along the giant rug laid out into a pathway decorated with rocks and a small creek, leading me through the giant playroom. Why was I here, though? What relevance did this place have to finding the-

Then it hit me again. I had to keep reminding myself that this wasn't a simulation. Not all the time, anyways. This was my subconscious. This was my memory. He was here.

I had to remember. I had to focus hard – closing my eyes – had to try my best to dig and remember the exact moment I spotted him those many years ago. Starting back from the theater, the house looking through the window, and then here...

Got it.

I crept over to the playground area, about the same size as one you'd see at any regular outdoor park. I climbed up the ladder leading to the three-foot platform, crossing over to the slide. I carefully stepped forward, squatting down slowly so I could peek my head into the opening, getting a good look through the tube.

No one there. Is that where I saw him? I thought so.

I stood back up, and across the distance by the giant porcelain giraffe, I saw him standing there behind, only able to see his head and feet as the rest of his body was blocked from my view. The bastard was behind me the whole time. I walked right past him on my way in.

The son of a bitch started running away, heading for another closed off play area, "Oceanville." Having no other time to take the ladder or jump over, I headed down the slide, which was surprisingly enough space for me to even fit, and raced after him. He disappeared into the Oceanville section, and once I followed inside the closed-off square shortly after, he was gone. I was only met with porcelain aquatic animals this time. Could he be hiding behind the blue whale? The orca? Maybe even the yellow submarine?

I wasn't going to bother falling into any of his traps. Jennifer mentioned before that I didn't have to see something I didn't want to. So I decided that I didn't want to keep playing this game.

I closed my eyes tightly, focusing not on a single word, but every thought about the man that I could muster. His height, size, what he might smell like, how he sounded. Whatever it took to get him closer to me.

When I opened them again, I was met with an entirely different place once more. An empty space that I could only describe as once being a library, ripped of most of its furniture and appliances. Only the check-out desk with a small Gateway 2000 model monitor propped on the end, screen entirely black, and a few bare, dusty bookcases stood present. The floor was partially carpeted with missing squares and badly damaged material. He was gone.

"Dammit!" I hissed.

But I quickly regained myself, as I realized where I was. The old public library back in Florida. He'd been here to. Again, I just had to remember where it was...

In the far corner stood multiple bookcases apart from the scarce amount on the side in which I stood, its own personal labyrinth. I'd have to go in. He'd be waiting.

Turning into the first row of bookcases leading into the maze, I noticed that these shelves weren't vacant like the others. There were rows upon rows of books lined neatly against each other, filled to the end of the shelf. I tried looking closely to see the titles or even authors of the uniquely colored reading materials, but alas, I knew that wouldn't work. How could I possibly remember every single book I passed by almost 20 years ago? As with the furniture and décor in Aunt Deborah's house, and the toys scattered across the floor of my old room, the books were unfathomable in identification. Could be looking at Shakespeare, Dickens, Seuss, *Junie B. Jones*...

I slowly turned the next corner, leading with my head as I did so. No man in sight. I kept on pushing. More books filled the shelves along the way, as well as a small apple figurine with an innocent, friendly-looking worm protruding from a tiny hole. I remembered that thing. It always stood out to me. I even asked the librarian if I could keep it, to which my mother insisted that that wasn't allowed, and that she'd get me one of my own. She never did.

A thump sounded from one of the other bookcases just a few rows down. I froze with dread, but hastily calmed myself as to not alarm Jennifer, taking fixed conscious breaths. My legs shakily snuck around to the path from where the thud was heard, and reaching the edge of the parallel bookcase, I leaned my back against the wooden furniture, carefully inching my head over to check. On the floor was a fallen blue paperback from the shelf, but no man. My eyes narrowed.

I picked the book up off the floor and turned to face its front cover. I grew wide-eyed from perplexity at the sight of the illustration and title, instantly recognizing it. *The Napping House* by Audrey Wood. Talk about a blast from the past. I was amazed at the detail on the illustration, mostly on how my mind could remember it so well. Perhaps it wasn't the most accurate depiction, but then again-

Ahead through the missing space on the shelf from which the book had fallen, the man stood on the opposite end of the case, eyes and mouth still unseen. This was it. This was the exact moment I saw him years ago. It all started right here…

He ran towards the left to try and make a quick getaway yet again. With all the force in my body, I shoved up against the bookcase, toppling it down onto the bastard. Countless novels, encyclopedias, essays, articles, all went crashing down in a violent mess. A chain reaction followed with the bookcases behind it, as they correspondingly toppled into one another like a domino effect.

I stepped down on top of the now fallen bookcase, peeking through the several empty sockets of hollow shelves. His body should've been there. I should be able to see through and find him lying-

From behind, the bookcase on the other side came crashing down, and I had no time to react. It was hard to say how fast it all happened, or if it was even still happening, but as the case impacted me, I was transported through the floor, making it shatter like glass, and all around me, the library followed suit, breaking into little pieces. As the current memory broke, I was transported back into the black stage void of my subconscious, watching as the fragmented pieces of the library around me, like tiny portals into a different dimension, began their descent into oblivion. Inevitably, I'd be met with the same fate.

I closed my eyes, ready to accept it. This is where I'd get lost in here forever, a prisoner of my own inner world. I would become a vegetable, never to utter another word or conscious thought again.

•••

"Travis!" Jennifer's voice called out.

My eyes sprung open, as an arm tightly clutched onto my own. I was hanging from an impossible height by someone's grasp, and when I looked to see who it was that saved me, I was quickly met with a sickness to my stomach.

It was him. He saved me. Why the fuck would he care?

I reached over with my other arm in a swift instinct to try and grab his face, that way I could possibly feel for a mask and snatch it right off his damn head. But the man was too fast, as he swooped me over the edge of the remaining carpeted platform from the library floor, with me barely missing his face. He pulled me right from his reach, just as he did years ago in the theater.

"Travis, are you there?!" she called to me again.

When I looked up, the man was gone again. I stood alone on the wandering platform in the black abyss.

"I'm here," I answered. "I'm here."

"Travis, where are you? What's going on?"

"I almost had him. I almost fucking had him!"

"I need to bring you back now! You've been in for too long."

"What do you mean? It hasn't been that long."

"Yes it has. It's been 45 minutes."

Christ, it felt like only fifteen so far. There was no way.

"I'm so close, Jennifer," I pleaded. "Please, you have to give me more time."

"I told you what was gonna happen. We had a deal."

"Please… just a little more time, please."

A brief moment of silence. I was waiting for it to happen any second now. In a moment, I'd be pulled back into the lab room where Jennifer would remove the Caduceus from off my head.

"Five more minutes," her voice finally replied. *"After that, I'm pulling you out. If I keep you past any longer, you may not come back."*

"Thank you, Jennifer," I said. Then I added, "It's flawed, by the way."

"What?"

"The Caduceus. The Hub. There's a huge error I'd like to point out as part of your feedback. Everything I'm seeing is supposed to be remnants of the past, pieces of memories I'd forgotten long ago or even more recently. You said the imagination is non-existent here, and that nothing can be replicated if it can't be remembered. That's false.

"Things happen out of my control. People from the past act independently on their own. I realized it with Tyler the second time I saw him in the Hub. I thought it was just a memory before, us playing hide-and-go-seek. But it was only half of a memory. I called his name once I realized it was him, and he responded. He looked at me. He hid behind me in terror as we were being chased.

"The man who kidnapped us. He's aware. He knows I'm onto him. That's why he's running. He can't do that if he's just a memory. No... it's more than that. In here, he's something more. He still lives here in my subconscious, freely. This version of him that I've created in my mind is real. And me... I saw myself as a younger boy. In the reflection. I spoke to him, and he responded. He told me what to do – *I* told myself how to play the game.

"And the book that I saw lying on the floor? I read that book years ago as a kid. It stuck into my brain after all this time. I never forgot it. I never forgot that cover. I remembered not only the picture on the front of the book, but the author. You said I can't fill in blanks that the brain can't truly recall, so how did that happen? I don't have photographic memory, Jennifer. I wish I did, but I don't. There's no way that picture should've been so clear as day to me! If I can't remember the faces of those people in the frames of Aunt Deborah's old house, then I shouldn't be able to remember that book. But how?!"

I aimlessly searched around, finding that the black void of space was no longer completely empty. Floating almost like giant hot air balloons, portal-like fragments of the various spaces I'd occupied throughout my childhood and adulthood drifted through the space, lonely sets and memories of long-forgotten seasons that I'd never get back. My eyes began to water.

It'd almost be nice to get lost here forever, I began to thought. I wouldn't mind it – being able to wander as I please through whatever memory I choose, forgetting and leaving all my troubles, consequences, regrets, and heartbreaks in the real world behind…

I'd be stuck down here with him, too, I reminded myself.

"But you were right about one thing," I said. "I don't have to see something I don't want. It's my subconscious. My mind."

I closed my eyes again, focusing hard enough to where I felt I could strain myself and burst a blood vessel. I opened them again, and there he was, right in front of me, back turned to where he couldn't see me. Before he could turn around in time to face me, I lunged forward, grabbing him by the neck. He struggled to fight me off, but he couldn't overpower me here. In fact, he had no power here. Not anymore.

In a brightly lit, colorful frenzy, the fragments of hundreds upon thousands of places and memories throughout my life began flashing around the both of us, like a rapid switching of TV channels down the guide. All moments from my life, in the span of seconds. And just before it all came to a crashing blinding halt, right then and there, I saw his face. The blinding luminescence overtook the area, overtook my vision, and soon after, the white light transported me back to the lab room, as the blurred view of Jennifer's face looked down at me through the headset goggles.

•••

For Georgia in the middle of January, the weather sure as hell didn't match. Bright and sunny skies painted the backdrop, complimenting the scenery as I drove down the decrepit pavement between the rich green meadow. Still quite chilly, as far as temperature goes, but I wouldn't have known that just by looking.

Tyler stayed in a small farm-type of home away from the city and constant noise pollution. Here, it was peaceful. It almost reminded of Florida a bit, which, I supposed, they weren't that far off geographically. He let me inside, offering me a coffee, to which I politely declined, taking up the offer of tea instead. I'd had enough coffee from Jennifer after waking up in a panic from the Hub.

In the middle of the kitchen, I sat at the table while he leaned against the counter across sipping his coffee.

"How're you holdin' up?" he asked frankly.

I shrugged. "All right," I answered, a lie, of course. "I'll manage."

He nodded. "Do you remember now?"

I returned a somber nod. "Everything," I said. "I wish I didn't."

"Me too."

"Tyler, I had no idea. I had no idea when I saw you again for the first time, the things you went through. I had no idea…"

He nervously tapped his mug, tightening his grip. He then took a sip of his drink, then swallowed.

"Therapy has been a big help," he responded. "But also, family and friends. Support. That's the biggest thing. Take all the love and support you can get. Don't push any of it away or think for a second you don't need it or can make it on your own, because you don't have to. Take it all in."

I fought the tears that tried so desperately to run down my face.

"I went back in the Hub," I told him. "I saw him again."

Tyler's expression instantly changed. It was hard to tell if it was one of nurtured dread or pure rage.

I continued, "I had to in order to catch him. We had to put him away for good. He couldn't do this to anyone else's kid."

He then spoke in a quiet but deadly tone. "Did it work?" he asked.

I nodded. "We have his face. The police have it. It's recorded. The Caduceus allows us to record whatever we see in the Hub. I could either choose to keep it confidential or share it. I had no choice. With the technology we have these days – the forensics we have, they'll find him in no time."

And with that, his expression changed again to a darkly satisfied, content demeanor.

"If it's okay with you, I mentioned your name as well," I added.

"Good," he said. "I'll be happy to give my statement."

We sat on Tyler's back porch made out of a nicely-built wooden deck, the chill yet rather soothing afternoon breeze brushing against my face. He pulled out a pack of Marlboro Reds, drawing a cigarette, then extended the pack out to me.

"You smoke?" he offered.

"No," I shook my head.

"Want to anyway?"

I smiled. "Sure, why not?"

I'd done it before several times from college dorm parties, hating it each time. But with Tyler, it wasn't so bad. For once, it was actually comforting. We'd talked for hours, reminiscing about the past, catching up on our current lives. I had many friends, many acquaintances through the years. But I'd forgotten how great it was to have a best friend.

•••

"Do you remember that girl I had a crush on back in first grade?" he mentioned.

"Who didn't we have a crush on back then?" I teased.

"Yeah, but this girl, the one with the pigtails and big purple bows on the ends?"

I had to think for a moment. "Francine?" I exclaimed.

"Yes! You remember her?"

"I'm picturing what she looks like… yeah, I do. Whatever came of her life?"

"No clue, haven't talked to her since." I chuckled. "But remember that time I said I was gonna ask her out and I asked you to like be my wingman and set me up with her?"

"Ask her out? To what? We were like children."

"I know, but you couldn't tell *us* that. We thought we could do no wrong, thought we were the shit."

I laughed. It was sort of the truth, more so for him than me.

"Anyways, remember what I gave you?" Tyler continued. "To give to her for me?"

I tilted my head, unsure. "You gave *me* something to give to her?"

"Yeah, a gift. Something sweet, you know, so she could have. And then maybe she'd like me. I mean, I don't think it worked, but still. Remember the flower I gave her?"

Then I remembered. Suddenly, I remembered that exact moment clear as day.

"Yeah," I said, smiling. "You did give her a flower."

Tyler laughed. "Gosh, I was such a romantic," he teased himself. "What was it, a sunflower, daisy or somethin'?"

I took a hit out of my third cigarette, then blew out into the cold air.

"A dandelion," I answered.

About the Author

From a very young age, Aaron Persaud has been able to use his imagination to make up stories out of practically anything, particularly in the category of tales that keep you on the edge of your seat. He writes and posts short stories regularly on sites such as Reddit and Tumblr. The stories range from horror, thriller, sci-fi, and most notably, the unexplained. The gift we share as human beings is that of storytelling, and it is our duty to continue telling them for generations to come.

Email:
aaronpersaud@ymail.com

Made in the USA
Coppell, TX
07 March 2022

74603809R00173